BAD DUCK

ABIGAIL STARK

This is a work of fiction. The people, corporations,
organizations, institutions, circumstances, and events depicted
are fictitious and a product of the author's imagination.
Any resemblance of any character to any actual person,
either living or dead, is purely coincidental.

Edited by Abbie Phelps
Book design by Jess LaGreca, Mayfly Design
Cover photograph from
https://www.stocksy.com/4846341/leading-forrest-lines

ISBN 13: 978-1-64343-608-1
Library of Congress Catalog Number: 2023907496
Printed in the United States of America
First Edition: 2023
27–26–25–24–23   5–4–3–2–1

Beaver's Pond Press
939 Seventh Street West
Saint Paul, MN 55102
(952) 829-8818
www.BeaversPondPress.com

For you, the reader. May your days be long,
and your summers be warm.
—Abigail Stark

I want to write.

I want to put words on paper like paint on canvas, a hundred featherlight lines of meaning etched into a page like all of eternity could be kept between the covers of a book.

I want my words to sing, to dance, to spin like lines of lights, pulsating heartstrings that beat with emotion. And over and over again, they whisper—

Listen.

—Ashley Albert

FRIDAY

It's 6:58 in the morning, and my eyes open like clockwork. I lie there for a moment before reaching down and unplugging my alarm clock, which is scheduled to go off a couple minutes later. Staring at the spot where daylight has already begun its spread across my ceiling, I think about nothing at all.

Rolling out of bed, I stand in an almost robotic motion. There's a pair of jeans on the floor by my footboard; I pick them up, sniffing them to make sure they don't smell too bad to wear, but it's just a habit—I already know they're fine.

I rip a shirt from a half-open drawer and pull it over my shoulders as I head downstairs, making a morning ruckus as only a teenager can. My mom always tells me I have no grace, but she's not mean about it—it's just the truth. She says the house isn't big enough for the three of us and my noise.

I come to a thumping halt at the bottom of the stairs, where I can see my mom sitting at the dining table like she does every Friday morning. I love her, but she's a bit puffy. I don't know how else to describe it. She's the best person in this house by far, but the years have worn her like the water rubs a rock in a riverbed. We don't talk a lot anymore, and I'm not sure whose fault that is. Probably both of ours, but there's no point in thinking about it.

Mom gives me a wan grin over a cup of weak coffee. "Morning, Sam. You're up early."

"Yeah," I say. "I guess I am."

"We're out of milk, so there's no cereal, but there's toast if you want that," she tells me distractedly, fingering the handle of her coffee mug. It's chipped and blue, and it's seen better days.

"Toast is fine," I tell her. I walk into the kitchen, a sad, galley-like thing that faces west and gets no sun in the morning. Retrieving a couple pieces of bread from the breadbox, I pop them in the toaster—an ugly old relic of the eighties, but hey, it makes good toast.

As I wait for my toast to finish, I pull my backpack from the couch and put it on. There's a coffee table to the side of the couch; a number of cards are scattered haphazardly across it, ripped from the envelopes they were mailed in. They're birthday cards, all decorated with variations of "wishes to the birthday boy" and brightly colored slices of cake or balloons.

Mom sees me looking at them. "Let's, uh, not worry about that right now," she says, standing quickly and coming over.

I don't look at her. I'm used to them by now. "Yeah. Let's not," I say.

Just then, I hear my toast pop. I pull the pieces from the toaster, slather them in butter, and head for the door as Mom calls out to me, "Don't forget to brush your—"

The second half of the sentence is lost as I shut the door behind me. For a second, I stand there on the porch, munching my toast in silence. It's a new day in Redford, West Virginia, but it feels like every day that's ever come and gone in this place.

It's a small town, haunted by the memory of the Mine that closed years ago. If things ever change, they change slowly. We have a bar, which doubles as the town's restaurant; the one movie theater is sad and dingy. What we don't have is cell reception. Cell companies have installed and installed and fixed and fixed whatever they claim is the issue, but it never seems to take. In some very patchy spots on Main and a couple streets over, you can get three bars. In most other places you get one, sometimes two if you're lucky. Time's forgotten the town and the town's forgotten the people. That's the circle of life, I guess.

My neighborhood is small but well kept for the most part. Closely mowed lawns boast a decorative ornament here and there, like the bench in my neighbor's front yard that no one ever sits in. I stare at this bench as I brush the last of the crumbs from my fingers, but that doesn't do anything for the butter, so I wipe away the residue on my jeans.

Hiking my backpack over my shoulder, I turn toward the side of my house and go to retrieve my bike, which is leaning against the peeling paint of the siding. Some teens here have cars, but most don't. My bike is okay; I think I've had it for most my life. It used to be too large for me, but now it's a little small. I don't care. Its dark, seafoam-green frame is a bit bent, and the seat's faux leather is worn, but it's got two tires and a gearshift that works most of the time, so I don't complain.

I don't have a phone, but I do have a watch. I don't need to check it, though—I can feel I'm a little late, so I hop on my bike and peel onto the sidewalk, heading north. It's the same motions every morning, feet pedaling as the air whistles across my cheeks and runs its fingers through my hair.

I ride through my neighborhood, which is just beginning to wake up, morning light streaming through the trees that line the sidewalk. This early, the air is quite warm, not yet hot—but it will be soon. Today's going to be one of those days where the air suffocates as the humidity drowns; I can feel it already in the way the sweat is starting to bead between my shoulders.

As I pedal, the tires on my bike wear once again against the sidewalk I've ridden as long as I can remember. I started riding when I was five, or six, or seven—some age where tumbles still didn't matter and scratched knees and palms were the mark of a well-spent day. Our neighbor up the street had a grandkid who had grown out of their bike, so they gave it to me. No training wheels, nothing, but I wanted the freedom that I knew came with having a ride of my own, whatever form that looked like, so that summer I taught myself to ride. It was a painful summer, but now that I'm eighteen and still without a car, I think it was worth it in the long run.

Eighteen, eighteen. The thought plays idly through my brain. My birthday was yesterday. *Yesterday.* The concept of yesterday feels so foreign, one day and a million years ago.

My neighborhood flashes by me as I continue to pedal. The houses are all little boxes set on their quarter acre. Most are well kept. Some aren't, but that's any neighborhood anywhere.

This town used to have a lot of pride, Peety tells me. *Used to have a lot of pride, indeed. And then the Mine went out, but I think we've done a decent job holdin' to what's left of it.*

"The Mine," people whisper. Not "the mine"—this is up-percase, you can feel it. It's taken on an almost musical quality, as if it's some sort of symbol of a better time or place. In a way, I guess it is. I was only a toddler when the Mine went out, but it's still the cornerstone of the local culture. Redford was fortunate; unlike most other mining towns, when the Mine left, we had another business step in to take its place. Now most people here commute fifteen miles south to Bronner. There, they're employed by a manufacturing plant that produces a competitive line of reasonably priced grills and smokers. It doesn't get much more American than that, does it? And Mine or no Mine, Redford people are a proud American group.

By now, I've almost reached downtown. I look down at my watch, a beat-up thing. Its dial tells me it's 7:17. I frown. I'm a bit late, but I can still make it. I peel to the right, passing a few more streets of the residential area before coming across Main.

Redford's downtown is everything you'd expect it to be. It's a couple streets deep and only about three blocks long. It's got all the normal small-town accoutrements, and at this early on a Friday morning, it's all but dead. Starting at 6:00 p.m., though, cars will line the sidewalk, left there by folks eager to catch a flick at the Searchlight Theater or get their fix at Danny's Bar.

I speed along the sidewalk, which I have all to myself, and slowly brake as I coast in front of a building at the end of a block. Unlike most of the other buildings on Main, this building stands alone, set off from the sidewalk. Painted above the glass double door, in tall yellow letters, is a sign that says "LIBRARY."

It's too early for the library to be open. Even if it were open, I wouldn't go in. I used to spend a lot of time there when I was younger, but not anymore. I guess that's a part of growing up.

I get off my bike and walk it to the side of the building, where a low line of hedges separates the structure from the sidewalk. On the other side of the sidewalk is a small parking lot with a handful of spaces. I rest my bike on its kickstand and crouch in front of the hedges, letting out a quiet whistle. "Hey, buddy. You in here?"

There's a low keening noise. Getting to my knees, I reach deep into the hedge, flailing around for a few long seconds and wincing as the sharp twigs scrape my bare arms. Finally, I feel what I'm looking for. I grasp ahold and pull my arms out of the shrub, hauling a small white dog out with me.

"You stuck again, boy?" I hold his face up to mine. He's that type of little white dog every old lady in the world seems to own, the kind with hair instead of fur and an unhealthy underbite. "You've got to stop doing this to me, or I'm going to be late for school." His brown eyes look placidly into mine as he licks me on the nose. I smile and let out a small laugh. "Come on, let's get you home. You're a mess."

Cradling Baxter against my chest with my left arm and steering with my right, I kick off the bike. My passenger smells terrible, like dog and dirt and heavy wet breath. I'm riding west now, back the way I came in. Baxter, hanging limply, makes a high-pitched whine as I veer left into my neighborhood. I turn onto a street a few blocks down from my house. If you didn't know the area, it could be my street. They all look the same.

I skid to a halt in front of a quaint home with a well-manicured yard. The gate in the backyard's chain link fence is ajar. I walk up the driveway and along the short concrete path that leads to the front of the house; then, knocking on the door, I wait. A few long moments later, a woman in her seventies with white hair and horn-rimmed glasses opens the door.

"Sam?" she asks. "I wasn't expecting you, especially this early in the morning." Her eyes catch my companion. "Baxter!" she exclaims. "Had he gotten out?" I nod as she throws open the screen.

"Hi, Mrs. Dean," I say as I hand over the dog. "Yeah, I found him by the library on the way to school."

She strokes Baxter along his knobby spine. "Baxter, you should know better! You're not the spring pup you used to be. And you, Sam . . . well, aren't you just a saint? Like father, like son."

It's a second before I can bring myself to smile politely. "Right place, right time. That's all."

"Well, even if that is the case, thank you so much for bringing him back."

I step down from the stoop. "I've got to head to school, or I'll be late," I tell her.

"Of course, dear." As I head down the driveway, she waves at me and calls out, "Thanks again!"

Hopping on my bike, I ride off toward the school. Pedaling northeast lot by lot, I speed past front lawns, sedans, hedges, and newspapers dropped at the end of driveways. I see it all, but I don't feel anything. I just keep pedaling.

In the distance, I spy a man. He's taking his sweet time with his morning routine of picking up the newspaper; a steaming cup of coffee sits beside him on the driveway as he unfolds the paper and scans the front page. I see this all from a half a block off, coasting closer every second. As I pull up in front of him and stop, he looks up from the paper, startled. This man doesn't know me.

"Hey, there." I swipe a thin layer of sweat from my brow with the back of my hand. Early as it is, the humidity is already beginning to get to me. "I didn't mean to surprise you. I just wanted to ask—do you know what your daughter is doing tonight?"

The man's expression shifts from surprised to taken aback. "Excuse me? Do I—do I know you?" he asks, confused.

I shake my head. "Uh, I don't think so. And, if I don't get going soon, I'll be late for school." He frowns, and I speed up the pace of my words. "It doesn't really matter who I am, anyways. I know your daughter—Chrissy. And I don't mean to ask you what she's doing tonight so that *I* can know—I thought *you* might want to know what she's doing. You should, you know, ask her about it. You should ask her what she's doing tonight."

Now he looks quite dazed. A couple seconds later, he gives a disoriented nod. "Okay," he says, clearly still confused. "I will . . . ask her," he finishes slowly.

"Great," I say, getting ready to pedal again. "You have a good one," I tell him, and I give a friendly little wave.

He puts his hand up, looking more like he's trying to block the sun than offer a goodbye.

I pass several blocks in my sweaty, blank-minded fugue state before sliding to a stop in front of the school. Everyone simply calls it "the school," but its real name is St. Joseph High School. Home of the Fighting Knights, and the locale I've sunk my last four years into. Well, not *quite* four years. Not exactly. And at this rate, I'm not sure I'll ever make it out.

I'm a little later than usual, so I park my bike in the bike rack. I don't use a lock; no one does. No one has a lock for their locker, either. It's just one of those places. An all-American high school in a quaint little all-American town. Perfect, perfect, perfect, if you don't look any harder.

It's the only high school I've ever been to, but I figure they're probably all pretty much the same. You have the sports kids, though the offering of sports at St. Joseph is pretty limited. I wouldn't call them "jocks"—none of our teams are good enough to earn that title. We went to State once for softball in 1994, and I've heard the plaque is still up in the girl's locker room. We have the nerds, who hang out after class and build their projects in the shop. We have the drama kids too, who put on a couple of shows a year. Those are a pretty big deal in Redford, but I'm not much for art; I don't know if the plays are any good or if people will use any excuse to get out of the house in a small town. You have the other stereotypes too, but none of that matters. At the end of the day, we're all headed towards the same place: nowhere.

I join the last couple straggling clumps of students as we make our way inside. The school building isn't large, just big enough to house the body of four-hundred-some students. The principal, Mr. Barely, announces our exact number every year on the first day of school, but, that's getting on to be ten or so months ago. *More than ten months,* I think. *Ten months going on ten years.* I can't remember back that far.

Here and there people raise a hand to me in greeting. Sometimes, I even nod back. The hallways are short, and the building feels like an echo chamber, amplifying and reflecting all the sounds until I feel claustrophobic. I don't stop at my locker; instead, I walk straight to my geometry class and sit down in my usual spot at the back. I always choose to carry my backpack to all my classes, though I couldn't tell you why. I guess some things we start doing and then keep doing because that way is all we know. I think this is true for a lot of things, actually— not only the reason I carry my backpack with me all day, but—

The teacher starts the roll call, interrupting my thoughts. "Sam?" she calls out. I listlessly raise my hand. "Ashley?" she calls again, but this time no one answers. She looks up from her clipboard, and her eyes find the empty seat two rows up from mine. "No Ashley," she mutters to herself. "Chrissy?"

We have a substitute teacher today. I haven't seen my regular first-period teacher in days. *You'd think this lady would know our names by now,* I think humorlessly.

The class passes in a blur of lines, angles, shapes. I idly doodle them all in my notebook. I've always hated geometry and I'm not paying attention, but that's my signature move these days.

When lunchtime comes, I eat in the parking lot, sitting on the curb. Every day, I'll do something different for lunch. Sometimes I sit with people. Sometimes I'll wander the hallways, looking, looking endlessly for something, anything—I don't know for what, exactly, but I know that I'll know it when I see it. Today I sit in the parking lot, watching the quiet scene play out in front of me.

Mom put a ham sandwich in my backpack before I got up this morning, the same thing I have every Friday. I think about my backpack on the couch and the table with the cards. Most birthdays, Mom cleans up the cards before I can see them. Not this one, though. She's distracted today. *Eighteen years,* I think. Legally an adult, but I don't feel much like a man.

I pull crumbs from the crust of my sandwich and feed them to the ants as they make their endless trek from some unknown, far-off location to the hole in the sidewalk. Back and forth they go, back and forth forever. I'm still feeding them crumb by crumb as something catches the corner of my eye.

I see movement in the grass to the side of the parking lot. I approach curiously, finding a bird who's hobbling sadly along the grass, its leg twisted at a strange angle.

Frowning, I lean in for a better look.

It's a starling, a beautiful little thing. Its iridescent feathers shimmer as they catch the midday light. I put out my fingers instinctively, as if I'm going to touch it; then, catching myself, I put my hand away. "Hey, buddy," I say softly. "Not feeling so good?"

The bird does its best to hop away. "It's okay, I'm not gonna hurt you." I pull crust from my bread and put it on the ground in front of the bird, who doesn't seem interested in eating. "What?" I ask with a soft laugh. "My mom's cooking isn't good enough for you?"

I want to stay and watch the creature, so helpless and mesmerizing. Instead, I stand up and head inside, leaving my lunch lying on the ground.

I need to talk to Vanna, the school secretary, so I make my way to the principal's office. Her full name is Vanna Clouster, but she insists students call her by her first name. "It keeps me young," she says. I walk up to her desk, where she's writing something on a notecard.

"Vanna," I say, and she looks up at me. "There's a bird outside. I think its leg is broken."

"Oh, poor thing." She stands. "Let's go take a look."

Outside, the bird is still hopping feebly. "What a shame," Vanna says, gazing down at it. "To spend your whole life flying, only to end up like this." She looks at her watch. "Lunchtime is almost over, Sam. You'd better go inside. I'll take care of our little friend here."

———————

The rest of the day passes in a blur. In English, Mr. Peters calls out a question on our current book, *Lord of the Flies*, to the class. "Can anyone tell us why, although he's throwing rocks at Henry, Roger chooses to not actually hit him with any of the rocks?"

This question is met with the usual listless silence. After a long pause, Mr. Peters tries again. "Anyone?"

I volunteer the answer in a vain attempt to keep the class moving. "Social taboos. Though they're no longer part of their old society, Roger still won't hurt Henry."

"Very good," Mr. Peters says, clearly surprised. I'm okay at school, but I like English. It's the only subject I have any real talent for. My grades in the rest of my classes are passable at best and skin-of-my-teeth at worst. I've never failed a class, but boy, am I trying—much to the chagrin of my parents. My dad, mostly.

Finally, the bell rings, signaling the end to another long day. I pick up my things and head outside, following the herd of students trying to filter through the front double doors and escape to freedom. However, when I walk up to my bike, someone is already standing there, waiting for me.

It's Shanna. Shanna Sommers lives across the street from me and one house down. Kitty-corner, you could say, in the house with the bench.

We stand there awkwardly for a long second. Shanna has big eyes ringed in too much eyeliner, giving her the vague air of a deer caught in headlights. She's almost pretty. Her hair is short and light, and she's rocking a forest-green bomber jacket with several pins and patches affixed to the front. I've always thought the patches belonged on the back of the bomber jacket, but I've never said anything.

"Hey, Shanna."

"Hey, Sam." Another awkward pause. "I . . . haven't seen you in a while, and I wanted to check in."

"You haven't seen me in a while? I'm pretty sure I saw you yesterday," I tell her.

Shanna frowns. "That's not what I mean, and you know it." A third awkward pause as she twirls her hair around her finger, as much as she can with its short length. I know she's working up the courage to say something.

"Look, Sam," she starts, falters, and then starts again. "I want to make sure you're okay."

I shoulder my backpack uncomfortably. "I am okay."

"I know you *think* you are. But, Sam . . ." she says, almost pleading. "I also know things have been tough, and—"

I put my hand up to cut her off. "Shanna, I'm *fine*."

It comes out harsher than I meant for it to, and she takes a step back. Sighing deeply, I say more softly, "I'm—I'm fine."

Slowly, she nods. "All right. If you say so."

A long second passes. "Okay. Thanks," I tell her. Shanna starts to back away, but then stops.

"I know you, Sam. And I know you're going to do what

you're going to do. But I mean it. If you need anything, just let me know. Please."

"I know. I know you mean it," I say, doing my best to mean it too.

At this, she seems almost satisfied. She nods, short hair swishing back and forth.

"Okay. I guess I'll . . . I'll see you around then, right?"

I put my hand up in farewell, and she turns away, backpack receding into the thinning crowd. With Shanna gone, I pull my bike from the rack and hop on, glad to be out of school and away from the people.

Shanna and I used to be close. When we were kids, we would draw in chalk on the road in front of our houses; our parents would tell us to *get off the street or you'll be hit by a car*, but we never listened. The summer before fourth grade, she broke her leg playing tag with me when she tripped over the hose in my front yard. She wouldn't talk to me for a month after that, but she came around eventually. And in sixth grade, in her basement watching old Michael Keaton Batman movies one Friday night, she was my first kiss. Well, technically she was my second—the first was Sadie Benson on back-to-school night the year before. But I liked the second one more, so that's the one I count.

Shanna is right, I haven't seen her in a while. I do feel guilty about it, but not guilty enough to change anything.

It's four o'clock, and I've got something I need to do a little after four thirty. I pedal back into town, which has started to come to life; I have to slowly weave through the pedestrians crowding the sidewalk before finally hopping off my bike and setting it against a storefront. My watch reads 4:32. I wait patiently, leaning against the brick as I watch the pedestrians live their lives.

A couple minutes later, a boy of twelve or thirteen walks out of the shop alone. He makes a motion to walk around me, but I plant myself firmly in his way. He looks up, startled.

"Put it back," I tell him.

His face contorts into a mask of alarm. "But I didn't—" he goes to explain, but I cut him off.

"I saw you take it. Put it back." The kid looks scared, but he darts back into the store. From the window I can see him take a half-melted candy bar from his pocket and put it back into the display. Then he runs out the door and down the sidewalk in the opposite direction, away from me. *Better half melted than nothing,* I think.

I take the long way home, listlessly cruising down side streets, idly watching the world around me. Friday nights like these, I used to have a lot going on, but now it's just this. Just me and the heat and my bike, coasting forever.

I get home at about five. Thumping my bike against the side of the house, I head inside to find Mom in the kitchen. "Hey, Sam," she says, brushing something off her hands and into a towel. "How was your day today?"

I shrug. "Same as usual."

"That's . . . good," she says slowly, seemingly unsure as to whether this really is a good thing. "Chicken pot pie for dinner."

I grunt. At one point, chicken pot pie was one of my favorite dishes, but now I'm ambivalent about it at best.

"Your father is out," Mom says. She looks anxious, but she's trying not to show it. "He'll be home Sunday afternoon."

"Oh, yeah. And until then, he's a call away, right?"

Mom looks hurt. It was a mean thing to say, meaner than I had meant for it to be. *A call away* is easier said than done in Redford. With the lack of cell coverage, everyone out this way has a landline, but even those only work if the person you're calling wants to pick up. At least on a cell you can text.

I think about apologizing, but I don't. Instead, I turn to go upstairs.

"I'll call you down for dinner," Mom says, her voice trailing behind me.

In my room, I close the door, fling my backpack into a corner, and flop facedown onto the bed. I don't think about anything—there's nothing to think about. Nothing that's *worth* thinking about, anyway.

Flipping onto my back, I turn my head sideways, looking at my windowsill. My cheek is pressed against my comforter, which is an ugly blue-and-black plaid pattern. It's too hot for a comforter; it's been too hot all spring. *A real scorcher of a year already*, Peety would say. But that's okay, because I don't sleep under the covers anymore. When Mom asks me why, I tell her it's efficient. There's no need to make the bed if you never really use it.

My gaze wanders lazily over the assortment of things on my windowsill. My "crap," Dad calls it. Papers and action figures, a radio, wooden knickknacks I made in shop class last year. I pick up the radio. It's a walkie-talkie, not for music. Though it's been dead for a long time now, I click the transmission button anyway in a staccato fashion, penning some gibberish in Morse code.

Mom yells up the stairs that it's time to eat, so I plunk the radio on the sill with a thump and head downstairs, where there's a pot pie on the stove. I shovel some of it into a bowl and get a spoon from the drawer.

"We have plates, you know," she says, watching me scrape my dinner from the serving dish.

"I know," I say, and turn to head back upstairs.

"Sam. Why don't you eat down here with me?" she asks softly. "Let's eat at the table."

"I can't. I've got tons of homework." Mom crosses her arms. "Yeah, Mom, tons of homework. We're reading *Lord of the Flies* in English, and Mr. Peters is making us all write a three-page paper on societal norms and how they define us as individuals."

"Fine." She puts a piece of pot pie on a plate for herself. "Good luck with the paper." There's an edge of something to her voice that I can't quite place. Sadness, maybe. Or loneliness.

I trudge back upstairs and sit hunched over my bowl on the bed. Turning on the TV with the volume low, I eat my dinner, letting the noise and light play in the background. I don't have a lot of good days, but this one has felt particularly down. I think about the bird in the grass at school, and it makes me sad. I remember what Vanna said: *What a shame, to spend your whole life flying, only to end up like this.*

My room is on the second floor of a house with no attic, meaning the roof is peaked; my space loses about a quarter of its volume to the slope of the ceiling. Even though the sun is starting to set, the day's gotten no cooler. The honeyed evening light that spills into the room seems to suffocate me. I crack open the window, though I'm pretty sure that's going to do nothing but let the bugs in.

I lie in my bed, the golden light illuminating lonely particles of dust that float in the still air like a lethargic ballet. In the background, I can hear a cult of night insects droning to each other in an endless cacophony.

It's a Friday night. I am eighteen years old, barely. I live in Redford, West Virginia. And, in this moment, I am the loneliest boy in the world.

———

It's nighttime. I'm in the woods. There's the sound of water in the distance. I'm on a dirt path that stretches, stretches, stretches into the darkness and the trees forever.

Suddenly, a flock of birds takes off. They're around me, everywhere, suffocating me with their wingbeats. It's noise, noise, noise, never ending, never slowing, building to a screaming crescendo, and then—they disappear, swirling into the night sky above.

It's quiet again, for a moment. Then, I hear it. A soft flutter. A heartbeat in the underbrush. I lean forward, my hands in the bramble. I pull them out, expecting to see a bird. Crippled. Lame. Instead, I find—

White plastic. It's dirty. A molded shape, conical with thin sides and a hard red nodule on the front, lying in my palm. I stare at it as I wake.

SATURDAY

I don't remember falling asleep the night before, but I must have—I wake up disoriented, slowly coming to consciousness the way someone would breach surface tension in a shallow pool. My bleary eyes open, and I find myself staring at my ugly checkered comforter. Bringing my hand to my face, I'm still confused from the strange dream, already fading, about birds and . . . *badminton birdies*, I realize groggily, wiping the drool off my chin. *Whatever. Dreams aren't supposed to make sense*, I think, and I try to forget about it.

I turn to look at my digital clock, but it's dead. I remember I ripped the cord out of the wall the previous morning, so I roll on my back and look at my watch, which says it's 9:48 a.m. Normally, I try to get up early on the weekend, but since I didn't set my alarm last night, today I slept until I had my fill.

Sighing, I plug the clock back in, then get out of bed, fully clothed. I consider putting different clothes on, but I don't. Instead, I take one last look around my room and close the window I opened last night. I'm not sure it'll make any difference—the inside of the house isn't any cooler than the outside—but I know my room smells like acrid sweat and dusty things, so I crack the window again anyways.

The house is still as I descend the stairs. Our staircase is lined in old striped wallpaper, this sickly rose, green, and cream pattern that alternates in stripes of threes. I think it must have been fashionable many years ago, but how many years, I don't know. A few photos are mounted on the wall in thick maple frames. *Back before frames were plastic,* Mom says, even though I don't really know what that means.

There's a note for me on the kitchen table. "Gone to Bronner. Getting groceries," it reads in Mom's tiny, scrawling cursive. "Will be back before dinner."

As usual, I have the day to myself. Though it's not like I have a lot in the way of responsibilities when my parents are home—keep my room clean for Mom, be quiet and stay out of the way for Dad. There's still no milk, so it's toast for me. I pop a piece of bread in the toaster, then hesitate and put in a second. It might be a long day.

I look out of the kitchen window above the sink, which is framed in curtains that remind me of a picnic blanket. They're checkered red and white and seem to go with the several chicken-themed knickknacks Mom has spread about the kitchen. Decorative chicken salt and pepper shakers. Chicken calendar, this month featuring a rooster in overalls. Chicken cookie jar, which I think holds dried black beans instead of cookies. I wonder whether the chicken–picnic blanket combo aesthetic is weird or not, but like my room's smell, it's been a part of my life for so long I'm not sure I even register it anymore.

My toast pops up; I butter one slice and jelly the other, staring out the window and leaning over the sink so it catches my crumbs. *What to do today?* I wonder. Over the wood fence that separates our backyard from our neighbor's, I can see the sky. It's the color of complete perfection, not a cloud in sight—the kind of horizon that looks like eternity stretched out on a lawn chair. I run my fingers through my hair, getting crumbs and jelly on the tips.

I don't have much going on today. Friday is my busy day, with Baxter, Chrissy's dad, and a couple other odds and ends. *The bird now too,* I remember. Saturday is pretty relaxed, other than one thing to do in the afternoon. *But that's ages away.* It's just past ten. I've got hours to kill.

This particular Saturday, we'll have a high of ninety-six degrees, already a hot day for the first week of June. Wind will be coming out of the northwest at a languid nine miles per hour. Tapping my fingers on the sink, I decide to visit the lake. Not Stevens Point Lake—I don't go there. Gooseberry Lake, to the southeast. I'd always thought a gooseberry was a made-up plant, just some name for a lake, until I saw something about gooseberry jam in a magazine. Boy, was I surprised. What a dumb name for a fruit. It doesn't look anything like a goose.

Back upstairs, I pull a faded pair of swim trunks out of the back of a dresser drawer. Mom is always saying she'll get me new ones, but she hasn't yet. Once I've returned downstairs, I dump all the books from my backpack. There aren't many, just one badly scribbled-in geometry textbook and a worn copy of *Lord of the Flies.* After filling a bottle with water and finding a pair of old plastic sunglasses on the bookshelf in the living room, I shove them in my backpack and set off.

———————

Redford isn't a large town by any stretch of the imagination, but there's even less to the south than there is to the north. Most of the few lonely businesses are closed, though some are still open, including a dollar store with a perpetually littered parking lot. Sometimes I wonder if people drive there just to throw garbage out their windows. There are some sewer grates in the parking lot, and once I saw a fox kill a rat by one of them. That made me feel weird—kind of sad, but also like it was ironic in a way? I'm thinking about this again as I cruise through the parking lot at single-digit miles per hour.

Something glints in the corner of my eye—when I come up on it, I find a can of light beer. The top is still sealed, but the tab's been cracked off. It must have broken off when someone tried to crack it open, so they threw the whole can out the window. I smile widely and toss it into my backpack. *One man's trash is another man's treasure,* I think, and keep pedaling.

Beyond the dollar store is an old Episcopalian church where they do bingo on Wednesdays. I don't know what an Episcopalian is, and I don't play bingo. I did go once with Shanna and her mom, though, years ago. I remember thinking it was such a funny way to spend a Wednesday night. The basement of the church was filled with circular plastic tables, folding chairs drawn up to them. The bingo itself was confusing and weirdly competitive for a game played in a church. Old ladies heckled each other from across the floor, and a disappointed buzz ran through the room every time someone yelled "Bingo!" I'd always thought to get a bingo, you had to get five in a row, but they kept playing games called "coverall" and "block of nine." Mrs. Sommers asked me a couple months later if I'd like to go with her again, and I said no thank you, Ma'am.

Continuing past the Episcopalian church is the road that takes you south. A little while along that road, there's a trailhead for one of the paths that loops around Gooseberry Lake. That's the way I usually take, but I don't today. Instead, I decide to keep pedaling until I find a new trailhead. Finally, I spy a cut in the undergrowth I've not taken before. *This will do,* I think, and steer my bike onto the path. Every day, I try to do something different, try to find new ways to fill my time. Most days it doesn't work, but still, I keep trying.

Steering my bike into the woods, I start on the path. I don't come across anyone else, but that's not surprising. This part of the woods is pretty secluded. I think people are beginning to get tired of summer, and the warm weather that would normally drive them to the water isn't such a novelty anymore.

The area around Redford is heavily wooded. The woods of West Virginia are scrubby places; sometimes I'll see photos of forests in other states that look almost regal, but they sure aren't here. In the forests around Redford, thick underbrush clogs the spaces between the trees. It's wild, like the forest is choking itself, fighting for air.

I do like the smell, though. It smells like the gentle decay of once-living things, like moss and wet and growth. When I close my eyes, just for a second, I can hear the birds sing and the wind rustle the trees, and the heat doesn't feel quite as oppressive anymore.

Turning around a bend, I coast to a halt where a rotten tree has fallen across the path. I gingerly pick up my bike, hike it over the tree, place it on the other side, and am off again. I keep pedaling, traveling quite a way until I come to the trailhead where I began. *Nothing to see here,* I think, and pedal along the path again until I find a short strip of rocky waterline. It's not much in the way of a beach—a stretch of coarse sand, a couple logs to sit on. I take off my shoes and socks, sit, and listen to the gentle lapping of the water.

The lake isn't huge; the coast parallel to me is maybe a couple thousand feet away. About a thousand feet to the southeast, a tiny island sits in the water. I don't think it has a name. It's only a couple arm-spans across and a short stone's throw long. Above it, I see two birds fighting in midair over something only birds care about.

I used to swim to the island on hot summer days like this one. It's a short swim. The water is far from clear, but it's cool and refreshing. Once, I swam to the island and found I had a leech on my leg. That was pretty scarring—I had dreams for a couple days afterward where I had to pull a leech the size of a dachshund off my arm as it squirmed and squished and fought to latch back on. To this day, leeches make me queasy.

I miss the island and the perfect summer days. I mean, we still have perfect days—just look at this one, aquamarine sky so clear you could cook an egg on the blacktop. But those were a different kind of perfect, perfect in more ways than the weather.

I take the beer I found and bury it at the edge of the shore where the waves lap over it, leaving the top exposed above the sand. *This should cool it down,* I think, and it does. A few minutes later, I dig it up and saw a big hole in the top with my house key. Sipping thoughtfully, I stare out across the lake. My eyes wander, then come to rest on the island. *It's close,* I think. *So close.*

I stand up and wade out into the lake until the water laps around my knees. I could swim out.

I'm young, maybe twelve.

"Betcha can't make it to the island," someone says to me—the voice of a fellow child.

"I can!" I protest. *"I just—don't want to."*

I don't go any further. *I'll save the swimming for another day.* I stand there for a second, take one last sip of my lukewarm beer, and return to the shore.

There on the beach, I lie on my back, eyes closed, listening to the occasional squalling of birds and the cyclical rolling of the gentle waves against the shore. I move myself down to the shoreline to stick my feet in the water, where waves lap against my toes and the tops of my feet. I don't really notice the heat. I've always preferred it to the cold. Heat sits on the surface of my skin, drawing out sweat, but it doesn't seep its way into my bones the way the cold seems to. Lying like this, I'm lulled into a kind of trance.

———

When I open my eyes, my watch says it's two o'clock, and I'm hungry. I sit up, feeling like I've rusted into place, and rub my eyes with the back of my hands. *I want a sandwich*, I think. Guilt pings in my chest when I realize exactly how much time I've spent here. I didn't mean to waste so much of the day like this. I should have been out, doing things, instead of lying here in the middle of nowhere passing time. *Bad duck*, I think. I'm angry at myself. Some days, I forget what my obligations are. But that doesn't make it okay.

I stand up from the beach and shake some life into my limbs, hopping onto my bike and pedaling back into the woods. It's quite a bit hotter now than it was earlier, hot and sticky-humid. I pause on the trail and pull my water bottle from my backpack, taking a few deep swigs and pouring the rest over my head. Drops bead on the lenses of my sunglasses, making them hard to see out of. Shaking my head like a dog, I pedal off again.

When I emerge from the trailhead, I head north, back into town. Every once in a while, a car passes. I coast in front of the dollar store where I found the beer can and the Episcopalian church with the weird bingo. I veer to the right and pedal hard, riding the ditch by the side of the road. Eventually, I come to the Big6.

The Big6 is my favorite place in town, not that there's a lot of competition. Everyone has their special spots, the lakeshore they like to lie on most or the deer stand in the woods they think is lucky. The Big6 isn't a secret place like that, but it is my favorite. I've been riding here on my bike ever since

I could make it that far. There's something magical about being eleven and biking to the store for a soda you buy yourself with your own money, even if that money is sometimes pilfered from the nowhere spaces between the couch cushions. When I was younger, I used to sit on the curb of the Big6 and suck Coke through a straw as the sun went down, smelling the fumes of the gas pumps and the musky sweet scent of the woods and the grass in the summertime.

Peety owns the Big6—to be more precise, he owns half. It's part gas station, part convenience store, and part auto repair shop; Peety takes care of the gas station and the convenience store while his brother Tim handles the auto repair side. I don't know much about it, and I try not to pry, but I know Peety and Tim have some personal differences and a relationship that can be described as lukewarm on its good days.

Peety gives me a hearty wave as I open the door, tinkling a bell that's mounted to the top of the doorframe. He's a shorter man with thinning white hair, dressed in a striped polo that's seen better days; he's in his sixties, I think, but I've never asked. As I walk in, he puts a faded paperback down on the counter. "Hello, Sam," calls out to me. "You out and about today?"

"Sure am," I respond. "I spent the day at Gooseberry Lake. It was nice. I've got the sunburn to prove it."

"You kids think you're untouchable, but you really should be using sunscreen. If you don't, you're going to be thirty and have skin like a leather shoe."

"Oh, yeah? You speaking from experience?"

"Wise guy." He cracks a smile. "What sass, you shouldn't talk to your elders like that. I'm going to have to tell your ma you've been bullying me."

Smiling back, I walk to the back of the store where cold-cut deli sandwiches are lined up formally in plastic wrapping. They're pretty disgusting, but I'm hungry and I want one anyway.

"Speaking of your ma," Peety follows up. "I saw her yesterday. She said it was your birthday. Why didn't you say anything?"

I shrug, but I'm behind a row of chips and he can't see me. I turn around and pull a bag from the rack. "Just didn't," I say, walking over to the soda machine, where I fill up my water bottle.

"Not very hygienic, you doing that. Might scare off the other customers." I look around, knowing full well I'm the only person in the store. When I go to pay, Peety waves me off. "One free lunch for the birthday boy."

"It's not even lunchtime anymore," I protest.

"Fine. One free sandwich and chips for the birthday boy. Is that better?" he asks.

I relent. It doesn't matter, anyway. "Thanks, Peety."

"Don't mention it." He rubs his chin thoughtfully. "Eighteen years. I don't remember ever being eighteen. Seems like a lifetime ago. Eighteenth birthday . . . that used to be a real big deal back in these parts. Coming of age." I unwrap the plastic from around my sandwich and make a noncommittal grunt. I've heard this speech at least a dozen times before. "At eighteen you could work at the Mine. Most kids finished out the school year before applying to work, but not all. A good number would roll right on up at five the morning of their birthday and have a job by six. Especially if their family had money problems, or if their pa couldn't work. Those were the days."

"Not sure I'd want to work in a mine," I say absently and munch on my sandwich.

Peety looks at me, thunderstruck, then shakes his head. "That's almost blasphemy. You kids. You don't understand it. The Mine was the glue of this place. Without it, we don't know who we are anymore." He shrugs tiredly. "I can't blame you; you don't know what you've never had. That's the way it is, I suppose." I open the bag of chips, which crinkles loudly, and he adds, "How's the sandwich?"

"Tastes like plastic," I tell him.

He smiles. "I bet it does." As silence falls, his eyes wander off into the distance. "The Mine was a strange place. What it meant to this town . . . it was the lifeblood of the community. Whether real or imagined, it had a kind of power. Redford wouldn't have existed without it; now that it's gone, we're starting to have a hard time existing at all. Plus, folks said all sorts of strange things would happen at the Mine. Some of them I don't believe, but some of them I saw with my own two eyes," Peety says, looking at me with a glint in his eye. "But, eh, you don't want to hear this old man's old stories."

"Please, go on," I tell him. "I could use some lunchtime entertainment." I'm sure I've heard this story before—at this point I've heard them all—but I don't mind hearing it again.

The smile returns to Peety's face. "Well, since you insist. As I'm sure you know, I worked at the Mine for years. The Mine was founded in the 19-teens sometime—can't remember exactly when." He pauses and scratches the bridge of his nose thoughtfully. "It's got all sorts of passages that are all used up or not safe anymore, tunnels that have been blocked off. They had big boards up in front of the mouths so you couldn't get in," he explains. "There was nothing behind that wood but dark, empty mining tunnel. Still, sometimes, if you'd go up to those boards and peek through, you could see a light. I swear on my life, you'd peek into them and there would be a gleam back there in the pitch black. A faint little light, but it was creepy as all heck."

"Woah," I say. "That is weird."

Peety nods. "Yeah, and the guys thought so too. There was a tradition of leaving out money. Every once in a while, someone would drop some coins in a can. These cans were everywhere—old coffee tins, mostly—and they were stuffed to the brim with coins and bills. Some of the money was old, from the late 1800s and early 1900s, but no one touched any of it. Once the money went into a can, it was sacred." He shakes his head. "When a can got too full to put money into, we'd put up a new can. There must have been a couple dozen of these cans around the Mine. I'm not sure how it started, but I guess it worked. Kept the lights in the tunnels, and the ghosties where they belonged." He smiles and waggles his fingers at me, making an *ooooh* noise. "Ghost stories. Gotta love 'em."

Then he frowns. "Except the bit about the lights. That part is true. And it *was* creepy. That's one thing I sure don't miss about the Mine. But, enough about me. How're you holding up?"

I shrug noncommittally, but Peety continues to question me. "You seen much of Shanna lately?"

"We don't talk much anymore," I tell him.

"That's a shame. You were so cute when you were younger. Remember when you were twelve or so and she bought that Icee? You went to take a sip, but you dropped it in the parking lot? I thought she was going to smack you."

"Yeah. And then you gave her one for free as a replacement." I'd forgotten about that.

"Eh." Peety shrugs. "Customers fighting out front would have been bad for business."

Just then, the bell chimes as the door opens—a gaggle of girls flock into the store, flitting through the aisles and picking things off the shelves. I recognize them all from school, and as they come up to the register, they smile at me awkwardly, saying hello. I say hi back, but they don't really look at me. I move out of the way to let them filter through the register one by one. As they check out, I overhear a snippet of conversation.

"It's too bad you couldn't come with us to the Point yesterday, Chrissy. It was a ton of fun, but it wasn't the same without you. Robert did a backflip off the cliff and I thought he was going to die! It was so scary. But fun! You have to come next time." I recognize the girl speaking as Elle, a senior, the same as me. *I haven't talked to her in ages.*

"Yeah," replies Chrissy, "I don't know how my dad even found out about it—he wouldn't tell me. It was weird. I'm disappointed I couldn't make it, but I'm still going to Mike's next weekend, so at least next week won't be a total waste. Can your brother still pick up drinks for us?"

"For sure," Elle says. The rest of the conversation is lost as she and the girls tinkle out of the shop, looking very much like a flock of brightly colored exotic birds.

Watching them go, Peety leans over to me. "What's going on with you?"

"What?" I ask.

"Just now. You had a weird look on your face. Like you were thinking about something."

"I don't know what you're talking about."

Peety puts his hands up in mock surrender. "Fine, I won't pry. I won't pry about Shanna, either. I only . . ." He trails off for a second. "I only wish you'd see friends who are your own age. I know you have them."

I take a swig from my water bottle as Peety looks at me, pleading expression on his face, but I don't respond. "Getting older isn't easy. Believe me, Sam. I wish it were," he says, chuckling. "But, it's not. Certain things do make it easier, though. A girlfriend, for one. That's a place to start. And a car." At this, he gives me a wink.

"Yeah. I wish I had a car too. But a girlfriend?" I shrug. "Not sure I have the time for that."

Peety smiles, but it fades as he wipes his hand across his mouth. "While we're on the topic of girls, mine's been giving me a rough go of it lately," he says distractedly.

I raise my eyebrows. "Mrs. Van Slyke? Wow, Peety, I'm really sorry to hear that."

He waves off my sympathy. "Nothing to apologize for. That's how it is sometimes. Marriage is . . ." He thinks for a second. ". . . tough, but it's never not worth it. You have the good times and the bad times, but at the end of the day, it's always the two of you and the life you've built together."

"Seems like you guys have, uh, more of the good than the bad," I tell him.

Peety gives a half-hearted smile. "Eh, everything's perfect from the outside looking in, you know. Life is . . ." He struggles for a moment. "Like a cycle, I think. The good and the bad, it all comes and goes in waves." Looking up at me, he says, "When I was younger and we'd just been married, I used to have all sorts of problems. Anger problems, attitude problems. You name it, I had it." He shakes his head sadly. "But Marianne stuck with me through all of it. She made me a better person. When you're married, you work on it together. The 'together' part is what's important." He stares off into the distance for a beat before seeming to refocus. "Got any advice?" he asks, surprising me.

"Jeez, Peety. I don't think I'm qualified to give advice about this."

"You come to me with your questions, always asking me all sorts of things. It's time I return the favor. And I know you have a way with women. Or, at least, you would if you still tried. Give it your best—you're a smart kid. If it's bad, I promise I'll tell you."

"Okay. That's fair." I consider it for a moment. "I know you've been working a lot of long hours—do you ever get out together? Go on, like, a date or something?"

Peety barks a laugh. "It's been years since I've been on a date."

"Well, maybe that's part of the problem. Maybe you're not getting enough—" I falter for a second, looking for the words. "Quality time together. Maybe try taking her to dinner, or the movies?"

"Yeah? You know, that's not a bad idea. Maybe I'll do that. Thanks, Sam. Who knows? Maybe someday you'll get yourself that girlfriend after all."

I laugh. "At this rate? Unlikely."

I stay at the Big6 for a bit longer before I head home. As I go to fetch my bike, I pick up Peety's glasses, which are lying by the side of the building.

"You're a lifesaver, Sam! I've been looking for these all day," he tells me after I return them. I tell him it's not a problem, but he still promises me a free sandwich the next time I come in.

"No thanks," I tell him. "One plastic sandwich is enough for me for a while."

This gets a laugh. "I'll give your compliments to the chef," he says with a wink.

————————

It's dinnertime by the time I get home, and Mom is just getting back from Bronner with groceries. I'm in the best mood I've been in for a while, for no particular reason. Mom asks me questions as I help load groceries into the pantry. "And what did you get up to today?"

"Not much. Went to the lake and hung out."

Mom stops unpacking groceries, and looks me in the eye. "You went to the lake?" she asks slowly.

"Yeah, Gooseberry."

"Oh. I see." There's an awkward pause. "And how was that?"

"Nice. It was . . . nice."

"I see you forgot the sunscreen."

"Yeah . . . I already got chewed by Peety. You told him it was my birthday?"

"I did. Your eighteenth, at that. He give you a soda or something?"

"No, a sandwich and a bag of chips."

"That was nice of him."

"Yeah. It was."

Mom asks what we should have for dinner, and we settle on spaghetti. The light is starting to fade outside as streaks of shadow begin to stretch their long fingers across the yard.

We eat on the couch, a faded green loveseat, and watch bad reruns of old Western movies until it's dark out. Tired from the sun and the biking and content from the spaghetti, I lie on my bed and fall asleep immediately.

————————

I'm in my kitchen. I'm staring out the window, looking at nothing at all. The moon is larger than usual. The night is still. It's just me and—

Noise. Static, coming from behind me. I walk to the living room, where blue-green light casts shadows against the walls. A TV illuminates the dark room. It's a game show, contestants on the screen.

As I watch, the picture morphs into an—

Old action movie, all gunfire and inaudible dialogue. No sound but the heavy static, crackling, crackling. The picture morphs again, into a wall of interference. I walk closer, searching, searching for a pattern in the nothingness.

I begin to hear something in the noise, cutting through the crackling. It becomes clearer as I move closer. It's a voice.

"Sam," it says.

SUNDAY

I wake with a start at nothing in particular, rubbing my eyes groggily as the details of my dream fade to consciousness. The bedside clock says it's 9:47 a.m. My room is hot and the air is heavy, light streaming through in swaths. As I sit up, my ugly nylon comforter peels off my back with an almost audible *schwep*.

I complete the daily ritual of hunting mostly clean clothing off the floor, then head downstairs. I'm dehydrated, and the faded wallpaper stripes of the stairway make my head throb. Groggily, I find my way to the kitchen where Mom is standing over the stove, idly drinking a cup of coffee and reading a magazine.

"A magazine, huh? I didn't know they still make those," I remark. I pull open a cupboard and fish out a coffee mug. Printed on the mug is a vibrant red cartoon rooster.

"Coffee?" Mom asks, distracted.

"No, thanks. Water is fine."

Folding up the magazine, she lays it back on the counter. "You have plans for today?" I think for a second as I run the mug under the tap. "We have cups for water," she adds.

I shrug. "I prefer something with a handle."

"So. What're you up to today?" she asks again.

"I don't know. Maybe I'll . . . bike around. See what happens. I'd say I'd do some shopping, but I think I've got twelve dollars to my name, so that might be tough." I realize what I've said and look out the window uncomfortably. A beat passes.

"Well. What do you have to buy that we don't have in the house already?" Mom asks flatly.

"Yeah." I down the water and put my mug in the sink. I look at it for a second before picking it back up, opening the dishwasher, and placing the mug in the top rack.

Back upstairs, I pick up my backpack from yesterday. The water bottle is empty, so I fill it in the bathroom sink. As the tap water runs into the bottle, I study myself in the mirror. Same brown eyes, same brown hair, maybe a little longer than usual. Still, I don't feel like myself. I used to look in the mirror and hear some little voice in my stomach go, *That's me.* But now when I look in the mirror, I don't feel much at all.

Water runs over my fingers, and I realize I've overfilled my bottle. I pour a little out before screwing on the cap and chucking it into my bag.

I take stock of my cash funds. I have five dollars in my wallet, a ratty thing that holds my student ID and an old receipt for a movie ticket I saw months ago. I pull it out, start to walk across the room to my trash can, then pause and drop it on the floor in front of me instead. I cross the room to an old cigar box that my grandfather, the one on my mom's side, gave to me years ago. From it, I pull out another five-dollar bill and three quarters. Yanking my hamper away from the wall, I rummage through my dirty clothes until I find one particular pair of jeans with two crumpled one-dollar bills in the back pocket. I then take my grand total of $12.75 and shove it in my wallet, in turn shoving that into my backpack.

I take the stairs by two and pass the kitchen, where Mom is still standing, drinking what by now must be a very lukewarm coffee. I hold up a hand. "I'll be back later."

"Okay," she says, not looking at me. I stand there for a second before I turn and head out. *Bad duck,* I think.

Outside, I stand by my bike and consider things. I have $12.75 to my name and only a couple of things to do today. The first thing is at about ten forty at the Episcopalian church, and if I don't pedal quickly, I won't make it.

I speed through the neighborhood, rows of houses quickly giving way to asphalt and the smattering of businesses that line the southern edge of town. I swerve in front of the church and drop my bike to the dying grass of its front lawn. My watch says it's 10:36—I'm here just in time. Using a side door, I let myself into the basement of the church. They call it the fellowship hall, if I remember correctly, back to that one time I played bingo here years ago. There's a murmur that's slowly getting louder as a large group of people approach the room. Lining the room's longest wall are plastic tables, on which rest platters of food.

I approach a plate of blond peanut butter brownies. Lifting it from the table, I put it in the trash, dish and all, then duck out of the basement and hurry back to my bike.

What to do now? I ask myself.

I start north, figuring I'll stop by the school. It's as good of a place as any, and besides, there's a T-ball game going on today, so there'll be plenty of people to watch.

It's getting close to noon as I pull up to the school. The parking lot is fuller now than it is on a school day; it's not a big lot, but people turn out for T-ball. Nothing better to do on the weekends, and it's a family affair. America's favorite pastime—for tykes, anyways. Grandparents turn out for grandkids, that sort of thing. I've never been much for T-ball, or baseball for that matter. I think that, for a sport, it's bizarrely repetitive. The innings and outings, the running and the hitting, it feels almost scripted. Don't get me wrong, I still used to play. Sometimes we'd get together on a Saturday evening. That was when it didn't get dark till nine, and the air was still and hot even past sunset; the dirt and the grime would get in your clothes and in your mouth, but you didn't care. I was even pretty okay at it, but I never really enjoyed it. I loved the summer, though, and being out in the wild of it. I guess I played baseball for the summer, not for the sport.

Thinking that, I bristle uncomfortably. *That was a long time ago, though. No use thinking about it now.*

Slowing down by the side of the school, I tip my bike into the rack. Shoving my hands into my pockets, I walk to the back of the school where the bleachers are packed with folks screaming at Carter to "Run, run, you've got it!" and at Tommy to "Get him out, come on, Tommy!" I walk to the field and settle in next to the bleachers, toward the back where I won't be noticed. Instead of watching the game, I watch the spectators. Most look to be the parents and siblings of the kids furiously battling it out on the field, but there are plenty of grandparents and even what might be an aunt or uncle here and there. The stands are packed, people squished like sardines in a tin.

I'm at a house. There are people everywhere, people all around me. The lights are dim and the music is loud. I'm holding a cup of something. Someone is talking to me.

"Do you think anyone at this party has ever been to California?" the person says.

"Why even ask? You know the answer is no," I respond.

I force the memory away and fixate on the game. Almost everyone is dressed in some variation of the two teams' colors—red and white for one, and green and yellow for the other. Just then, a roar goes up from the green-yellow spectators. One grandma stands up and yells, "Way to go, Alex!" She has a heavy fob of keys in her back pocket, half of which are hanging out. As she stands, they slip from her pocket and fall through the bleachers, haphazardly clanging off a rung. Unnoticed in the noise of the game, they land in the grass.

I watch, interested. Then, a lady in a baseball cap and a red T-shirt taps the grandma on the shoulder and motions to the ground below. The grandma looks down with a start, thanks the lady in red, and excuses her way down the bleachers.

I sigh and settle back in, idly picking at the grass to at least keep my hands busy. Half an hour passes and they're in the fourth inning with nothing else of note having happened on the people-watching front.

My stomach grumbles, and I grimace. Not eating breakfast this morning was a mistake, but I wasn't going to stay in the house any longer, not after that uncomfortable exchange with Mom. There's a hot dog cart at the game, a little stand operating to "Benefit Redford VFD," as explained by the side of the cart itself. I order two hot dogs.

"That will be two dollars," the hot dog cart operator tells me. He looks ex-military and like he very much does not want to be there. I hand him the crumpled bills wordlessly. With crisp motions, he takes them both, makes a show of flattening them on the counter, puts them in the cash box, and hands me two hot dogs wrapped in napkins. I mumble my thanks.

"Fixings are that way," he says, pointing to a short table where a girl is methodically pumping ketchup onto a hot dog that's already drowning in the condiment.

The girl's hair is dyed black, worn in a high ponytail. She has a red-and-black flannel button-up tied around her waist, like she took it off when she decided ninety degrees was too warm for a second layer. Her jeans are torn, though they don't look like they were bought that way, and she's wearing a T-shirt from a band I don't recognize. I recognize her, however—Ashley Albert. *She's always absent on Friday.* She glances at me quickly, hand still pumping the ketchup dispenser.

I decide to say something. "You want some hot dog with that ketchup?" I joke, trying to be friendly.

She looks up at me again, this time pausing her motion. "No," she says, then goes back to the ketchup.

I've never talked to her much at school. Though we're in the same class, she seems younger. She's smart, but very quiet. *She doesn't have a lot of friends*, I think, and try again. "You weren't in school on Friday," I tell her, trying to make conversation.

She stops pumping, stands up tall, and peers at me, wiping a stray piece of hair off her forehead with a ketchup-streaked finger. "Why do you ask?" She doesn't say it in a rude way, but rather like she's curious.

I'm surprised by the question. "I don't . . . mean to be rude," I tell her. "I just want to ask if you're okay."

She nods slowly, as if she's deciding whether I'm being earnest. "I'm fine. Thank you."

With that, she steps away from the table; then she turns around and makes her way back to, then past, the baseball field, where she disappears behind a second small food cart. If I squint, I can make out the noble cause the second cart seems to be serving: "Support Uganda Missionaries."

That was weird, I think, and take a bite out of my own hot dog. I grimace a little when I realize I've not put ketchup on it yet—hastily, I run it under the dispenser. Looking up, I catch the eye of the ex-military type, who's looking at me disdainfully.

"Unhygienic," is all he says.

I nod slowly and retreat from the ketchup, my second dog still plain.

Sighing defeatedly, I walk back to my bike. I take a bite of my second, plain, lukewarm hot dog and think to myself, *Another day in paradise.*

I make my way back to my bike and decide to head downtown; maybe I'll find something there. At this point, it's already past two, and the humidity is palpable. With every pedal, it feels like I'm cutting my way through the atmosphere. I'm sweating through my dark blue T-shirt. "Redford Patriotic Days," it says on the back—an old shirt from a Fourth of July parade I volunteered in years ago. I can tell my sunburn is getting even worse, but I don't have it in me to care. It'll be gone by tomorrow, anyway.

I coast downtown, dodging groups of people walking here and there along the sidewalk, and stop in front of Danny's. Everyone thinks of Danny's as the bar, but they have food, so it's technically a restaurant. Being underage, this is an important distinction to me. *Eighteen, eighteen. Could work in the Mine, but still can't get a drink,* I think dryly. *Legally, anyway.*

The exterior of the building is rustic and wood paneled, a theme that continues into the inside of the bar. *Restaurant,* I mentally correct myself. The food is pretty terrible, though, so most people visit Danny's for the attractions of the liquid variety. Neon signs advertise craft beers and non-craft beers alike. In the back, there are a couple pool tables. I don't play the sport, if you can call it that, and at this point in my life I feel simultaneously too old and too young to start. Instead, I veer toward the counter, where I'm greeted halfheartedly by a waitress in a black tank top whose makeup is sliding off her face in the heat. If Danny's has working air conditioning, they sure aren't using it, and the lone fan turning lazily in the rafters isn't working any magic.

The waitress looks me up and down as she leans against the bar. "What'll it be, honey?" she asks shrewdly.

"Just a large Coke," I say. "To go, please." She nods en-thusiastically, seemingly happy I'm an easy customer and not some obviously underage kid trying to pass her a fake ID for a lukewarm whisky at two o'clock on a Sunday in an empty bar. As she walks lazily to the back to get my order together, I take a seat on a stool.

I imagine being here in six or seven years, shooting pool in the back. In this make-believe world, I've picked up the sport, and I'm pretty good at it. I'll get another beer from the bar—maybe a shot of vodka, or even tequila, if it's early and I'm feeling adventurous. But not a bourbon, never bourbon, because that's what Dad drinks. I'll chat with my friends, with the girls, and I'll play pool, and it'll still be meaningless, all meaningless, one speck of dust in a cosmic ocean of nothing that doesn't care about anyone or anything. And the beer and the pool are just the icing on the cake, trying to cover up all the little cracks in everything. Not that it matters if nothing matters, because who says I'll even make it to twenty-five?

I realize I've been nervously combing my fingers through my hair and take my hand away from my greasy mop as the double doors to the back swing open. The waitress slides a large Styrofoam cup to me. "No minors at the bar," she says, and I stand awkwardly from the stool. "That'll be one-fifty. You need a receipt?"

"Ah, no. I don't," I tell her, fishing a five from my wallet and handing it over. She lackadaisically breaks my bill, and I leave two dollars at the counter.

I stand to leave, but something catches my attention as I turn to go. There's a thin square of plastic that's adhered itself vertically to the base of the bar by the floor. I pull it off and realize it's a driver's license, glued by some gross, mysterious substance to the bottom edge of the bar.

"What'cha got there?" the bartender/waitress asks me.

"Just dropped something," I lie, heart beating quickly as I pocket the license and head outside.

Standing on the corner, I eagerly pull out the license. "Kathleen Sherman," it reads, with an address right around the corner. I quickly do the mental math. *Her twenty-third birthday was last month,* I think, for no reason at all.

I pedal down the street a way, turning a couple corners until I'm in front of a house sporting an averagely manicured yard and a beat-up sedan in the driveway. Walking up to the car, I slip the license under the windshield wiper, then return to my bike.

————————

I end up visiting the hardware store—nothing else to do. On a whim as I'm leaving, I buy some batteries, which I shove into the bottom of my backpack. I'm already regretting the purchase as I walk out through the doors, but it's too late to think about it, so I don't. Instead, I look at my watch. *Perfect timing.*

I hop on my bike and pedal to the residential area that parallels downtown, cruising the sidewalk before dropping my bike under the shade of a large tree whose boughs overhang the pavement. I sit under the shade and idly watch the occasional car trickle by.

Right on time, a little boy rounds the corner in a faded striped T-shirt. He can't be older than four. He looks dazed.

"Hey, there," I call out. "You lost, buddy?" He whimpers and his face puckers, looking like he's about to cry. "Hey, no need for that," I tell him. "Let's get you home, okay?" He nods.

I know where he lives, a handful of streets over and a few houses down. We make small talk as we slowly trudge along the sidewalk. "How about I guess your name?" I ask him.

"Okay," he says.

"Paul?"

"No."

"Bartholomew?"

He giggles. "No."

I'm at school. It's lunchtime. I'm talking to a friend.

"My sister got a cat last week," my friend tells me.

"Yeah? What's its name?" I ask.

"Kevin," they say. I snort so hard milk comes out of my nose.

A third voice chimes in, also laughing. "Who names their cat Kevin?"

I shut the thought out, focusing on the sidewalk and the boy beside me. "T-Rex?" I ask.

"No! That's a dino-sear." He can't quite figure out the pronunciation of the word *dinosaur*, but he gets it pretty close.

"Ryan?" I ask.

He looks up at me, wide eyed. "Wow," he says. "That's my name too."

I don't think he quite gets the point of the game I was trying to play, but it doesn't matter. We've arrived at his house.

I walk him up to the front door, let him inside, and close the door again, waving goodbye to him.

I return to my bike, which is still sitting under the tree. I wonder where to go next, and figure it'll be time for dinner soon enough. But until then, I might as well take my final two dollars and go see Peety.

Hopping on my bike, I make my way east, the stale midafternoon air pressing against me as I pedal to the Big6. I drop my bike outside the door and head in, Peety looking up at me from behind the counter. "Hey there, Sam. You're looking a little worse for wear."

"That bad, huh?"

"The sunburn doesn't help much. You been out all day again?"

"Sure have, Peety. Too much to do and not enough time."

"Oh, yeah?" he says, leaning on the counter and raising an eyebrow. "And exactly what all did you have going on today?"

"Well, I went to the T-ball game this morning, where I ate not one, but *two* hot dogs. Then, I had a Coke from Danny's and went to the hardware store." I tick all these things off my fingers like they're accomplishments.

"Hmm. The exciting life of a teen in Redford."

"And now I'm here to kill some time before I go home. Mom is making tacos for dinner."

"Taco night? Lucky."

I shrug. "Every Sunday is taco night, these days."

"Speaking of dinner," Peety says, "guess who's going home early tonight to cook for the missus?"

"Hey! Nice. You're taking my advice from yesterday?"

"I sure am. I'm going to surprise her with my grandma's classic spaghetti and meatballs, and a bottle of wine."

"Oh, yeah? And how long has it been since you've made that recipe?"

Peety crosses his arms in thought. "It must be going on fifteen years now."

"Well, I hope you've got it written down somewhere."

"Probably, in our recipe box. And, if not, how hard can it be? It's only spaghetti."

"And meatballs," I remind him.

"Right, and meatballs. But hey, isn't it the thought that counts?"

"Right. Who've you got watching the shop?"

"Martin. I'm going home at six thirty, so he'll be coming over to man the counter and close up. It'll be a late dinner, but better late than never." Martin is Peety's nephew; he works at the attached mechanic shop and covers for Peety when needed.

For a few moments, Peety looks at me, as if considering something. "You know," he says slowly, "Martin can't be here to cover for me all the time. If you're ever interested, that offer of a job still stands. It might help take your mind off—"

I put my hand up abruptly to cut him off. "I appreciate the offer, Peety, really, but I think I'll have to pass for now. What can I say? My weekends are pretty packed already."

He snorts. "Yeah, yeah. You've got hot dogs to eat and hardware stores to visit. Keep it in mind and let me know if you ever are interested. I could use the part-time help." A moment later, he softens up. "You're a good kid, Sam. And you spend a lot of time here. It wouldn't hurt you to get paid for it."

I nod but don't look at him, instead walking to the back of the store. *What to buy, what to buy?* I settle on a bag of chips and bring them to the counter. Peety raises an eyebrow. "Hot dogs, a Coke, chips, *and* tacos? You might have to watch your figure. No charge, though, since you found my glasses yesterday."

"Thanks. But, hey now—you burn a lot of calories when your primary mode of transportation is a bike."

"Fair enough, that's true." For a second Peety is quiet; then he looks up, peering at me intently from behind his glasses. "Sam, I worry about you. I think you know that."

I shake my head. "Peety, don't. You really shouldn't."

"But I *do*. Your only friend in this town shouldn't be an old man like me. I know things haven't been easy for you, and I know I said yesterday that I'd drop it, but—you should have people you can talk to. Someone who's your own age. You used to have so many friends—what happened? I wish you'd reach out to someone. Someone like Shanna, maybe?"

"I talked to her Friday," I say, which is not a lie but also not quite the truth.

"You did?" Peety says, surprised. "How is she?"

"Good. Same old, same old," I say, something I assume rather than something I actually learned from the conversation. *The conversation that sounded a lot like this one,* I think, but I don't say it. Peety looks satisfied, so I change topics.

We chat for a bit longer after that. I don't have a lot of adults in my life—not a lot of people in my life in general, anymore—but talking to Peety is easy and comfortable. *For the most part, anyway,* I think. I don't mind that we always seem to talk about the same things. Well, the dinner with his wife is new, I guess, but I'm glad he's doing it.

We talk about the town and the weather. Peety tells me about his grandkids and his car that needs work, which is ironic given that his business is attached to an auto shop. Periodically, our conversation is interrupted as people come through to buy this or that or to put twenty on pump two; then we return to it, as if no time has passed. Eventually, though, the effects of the chips and the Coke wear off, and it's time to get home for dinner.

"Good luck with Mrs. Van Slyke," I tell Peety as I stretch and rise to leave.

"Sure, Sam. Hey—before you go, do you know any tricks for a good spaghetti?"

I think about it for a second. "Salt the water? I've heard that tip."

Peety nods, satisfied. "Have a good night."

————————

I wave to Peety as I pick my bike off the curb and begin to pedal home. The sun is setting, starting to bathe the forest and the road and everything in between in a thick, sticky honey glow. I think about Peety's dinner with his wife. They live a handful of streets down from me, which isn't surprising. Redford isn't a big town, so if you don't live in the woods to the north or the south, odds are you live a few streets from yours truly.

Soon, I'm standing my bike up against the side of the house. Mom looks over to me as I push the front door open. "Hi, Sam. How was your day?"

"It was good. How was yours?"

She shrugs. "Fine enough. We can talk about it over dinner. I made tacos. Do you want to eat?" I help her bring the food to the table.

"Will you put out the plates?" she asks. I pull two dishes from the cupboard and set them at their places.

"Will you set a third?" Mom asks.

I look at her, then back at the two place settings. I pull a third plate from the cupboard and set it on the table with a dull thud. Neither of us speak for a second.

"Great," she says, her voice suddenly uncomfortable. "I'll get the silverware." We sit at the table to say grace, and I pile toppings into my shell like it's the first food I've had in a week. "Tell me about your day," Mom says, trying to make conversation.

I shrug. "Stopped by the school for a bit, watched the T-ball game. Went downtown, visited Mr. Coen's hardware store."

"Mr. Coen is a nice man. A little odd, but nice. I haven't been to the hardware store in ages, though. I don't know if you can really call it a hardware store—he seems to have a little bit of everything. Still, these days, I only ever seem to shop in Bronner." There's a lull in the conversation. "Did you see his curio cabinet?" Mom asks.

"Yeah. He's got some weird stuff for sale."

"Last time I was there, and this was at least a few months ago, he had an entire deck where all the face cards had been painted to look like Bible characters. The queens were Mary, the kings were Jesus—I don't remember who the jack was, though."

"You can't play poker with that deck," I comment.

Mom smiles thinly. "No, probably not. You see Peety today? I know you stop at the Big6 often," she asks, trying to keep the conversation alive.

"Yeah. He said he's surprising Mrs. Van Slyke with dinner tonight."

She arches an eyebrow. "Oh, yeah? Did he say where they're going?"

"Peety's cooking," I say.

Mom frowns. "I bet Peety hasn't cooked a meal in ten years."

I think back to our earlier conversation. "It's been longer than that, I think." I push my chair from the table. "Thanks for dinner, Mom."

Mom checks her watch and anxiously runs her fingers through her hair. I frown. I have the same nervous habit, and it's strange to see it worn on someone else. "Tomorrow is a school day. Don't stay up too late, okay?" she asks.

"Sure, Mom. I won't."

Upstairs, I open my backpack. In the front pocket is seventy-five cents in loose change, which I set on the windowsill next to my bed. I pull out the four-pack of batteries I bought from the hardware store, staring at it for a second before I rip open the back of the carton. Plucking my walkie-talkie radio off the windowsill, I take off the back panel and pop out the four old batteries, which I toss across the room and into my trash can. Only two of them make it into the bin, but I leave the ones I missed lying on the floor. I slide the new batteries into the back and replace the panel.

Like I breathed life into it, a faint green LED at the top of the radio begins to glow.

The radio makes a static crackling noise, which I turn down until it's barely audible. Its weight is familiar in my hand. I press the transmission button, and the crackling static goes silent. *Bad duck,* I think.

Suddenly, I turn off the radio and set it on the sill before quickly moving to pick some comics from my bookshelf across the room. I'm not much for comics, but I have a few. A couple years back, this guy named Brian Malone lent me a stack. Then his dad got a job offer in another state, and his family moved. No one gets out of Redford, but Brian did—and fast. He was in school on Friday, then never came back—they moved that suddenly. I figured the comics were mine.

Turning on the lamp on my bedside table, I flip through a comic for a few minutes. Then I stand up and go to the kitchen, getting a mug and filling it from the sink. The stove clock says it's 8:48 p.m., and it's starting to get dark outside. Mom is watching TV in the living room. I move to go back up the stairs when she calls out to me.

"Take a shower, please, Sam. I could smell you across the table, and you never get up early enough to shower in the mornings."

I roll my eyes. Shower or no shower, it makes no difference. But it will help pass the time, so there's that.

Later, I'm having a hard time sleeping. This happens sometimes, even when I've spent all day outside in the sun and on my bike. The sad irony is that sometimes I'm at my most physically exhausted when it feels like my brain is on fire thinking, thinking, thinking. I toss and I turn—try to think about nothing, about the comics and school—but it doesn't work. The thoughts still creep in on me from the edges. The thoughts I try to avoid, to shove deep, deep down and back into the crevices of my mind. *Bad duck,* they say to me.

I'm hot and tired and still clammy from the shower. I doze shallowly for a few minutes at a time, but when I wake, it feels like I never slept at all. The alarm clock says it's forty minutes later, but I'm as awake and exhausted as ever.

I kneel on my bed and slide the window open, pressing my face to the screen. Breathing in the sticky night air, I feel a little better. I've given up on sleeping, so I slide on my clothes and creep down the stairs. Mom has fallen asleep watching TV, the bright light from the screen bathing the living room in a green electronic glow. As quietly as I can, I slip out the front door and pick up my bike from the side of the house. I walk it to the road, my eyes adjusting to the dark of night.

———————

I start to coast down the road, slowly at first. I head north, pedaling in the middle of the street, the way I do some nights when I can't sleep. No one is out this late; it's only me and the occasional streetlight. I can hear the night critters chirping and mewling their night songs, individually quiet but together a cacophony. They scream into the night, into the void. The street is dark, but it's alive, and I have plenty of company.

The air lies heavy and thick upon the evening. It's a cloudless night, and up above I can see the twinkling of the brightest stars that are able to fight their way through the light pollution, thin as it is in rural West Virginia. The night air fills my nostrils; it's hard to explain, but it smells like night in the way the world smells like rain after a downpour. It's damp and dense, restless and a little lonely.

I start to pedal faster, and faster, and even faster still, the rush of wind in my ears melding with the screams of insects until the world is a wall of noise. All I can see is the cycle of dark, light, dark, as I come upon and then pass streetlight after streetlight. I don't know how fast I'm going—maybe thirty miles an hour, but it feels like three hundred, pedaling with reckless abandon as the wind screams in my ears, headed into the inky, hazy black night.

I'm coming to the edge of town—I can tell because I see an end to the line of streetlights. I start to slow, and from the end of the lane, a car turns onto the road. I brake to a halt and pant for breath, realizing how winded I am. I pull to the side of the street to let the car pass, headlights blinding me momentarily. Then I turn around and began a slow pedal home.

I slide through the thick night like a ship through the water. I pedal lazily, relishing the feeling of the air and the noise and the seat I'm sitting against. It feels good to be so present. I'm usually lonely, though not alone, but when I'm alone like this it's a lonely that feels right. Comfortable. It's hard to explain, like it's just me and the stars and the bugs and the breeze, and that's okay. I feel like it could always be night—if I pedal and pedal and run and run it'll be night forever, and I'll be okay. I take a deep breath and slide through the night in a comfortable fugue.

I come to, however, when I notice a house I was too busy streaming by earlier to register. The other homes on the street are closed up, with just the occasional flicker of a TV or a night-light to breathe life into them. This house is a beacon, lit up like a mono-color Christmas tree, looking like every bulb in the place must be burning. Curious, I cross the road to get a better look. From the front, I don't see anything strange. I consider moving on, but instead, I drop my bike in the yard and creep to the side of the house.

As I move in closer, I can hear an agitated voice. The thin, single-paned glass means the details are lost to the general warble of the—*conversation? Argument?* I'm not sure. Coming around the corner of the house, I finally get a good look into the kitchen, where there are two people sitting at a dining-room table. Those people are Peety and Mrs. Van Slyke.

I step back, startled. I don't know what I was expecting, but it sure wasn't this. My actions suddenly feel a lot less like curiosity and a lot more like eavesdropping. Still, I stay for a few seconds longer. The more I watch, the more alarmed I become.

Mrs. Van Slyke has her head in her hands. Peety stands, clearly restless, then sits again, seemingly to implore Mrs. Van Slyke of something. His body language is clearly desperate, and hers seems . . . *scared? No*, I think, *that isn't it. Anguished.* I can see her shoulders heaving—she's crying heavily.

I creep closer to the window, nose almost pressed to the glass. They'll see me if they look up, but they never will—what's happening between the two of them is so intense they've gotten lost in it. Though I'm focused on the scene in front of me, I can't help but catch details of the house. The dining room is clean and presentable in the way it feels like all grandparents' dining rooms are, with dark colors and a tablecloth. On the table is a dinner that looks like it's been sitting out for a while. Piles of largely untouched, rubberized spaghetti languish in congealed sauce on the plates. Also sitting on the table are two full glasses of water, but the center is commanded by a bottle of wine. One wine glass has tipped over, dark liquid soaked into the already dark tablecloth; the other sits full and untouched.

Peety is sitting now, and I'm close enough to hear the details of their conversation. "All these *years*, Marianne. All the *years*, all the *kids*, Marianne. And what am I supposed to do? What am I supposed to do with this?"

She looks at her hands, then back at Peety. Her eyes—no, her whole face is red and puffy. Her hair, which is usually swept up in a prim, gray bun, is coming out of its holder in sheets and plastering itself against her face, wet from the sweat and tears. Mrs. Van Slyke usually carries herself with grace and dignity. But here she sits, compressed. Smaller, somehow.

She takes one shaking hand and puts it against Peety's forearm, saying something quietly that I can't make out. Peety stands again.

"Don't *tell* me that. This is our life. Here, in Redford. I'm too *old* for this. Aren't you?"

Pressing a napkin to her mouth, she chokes something out, as if she's in pain. Peety stays frozen, every muscle in his aging body tensed. Finally, he runs his hands over his face in anguish and frustration.

"How long, Marianne. How long?" Mrs. Van Slyke says something.

"That's not an answer! We've been married forty-some years. Don't you think I deserve more than that? More than *this*?"

Mrs. Van Slyke says nothing, just cries into her napkin, which doesn't look like it can take any more crying, lump of pulp as it is.

"It's been *hours*, Marianne. We get through things together, it's what we do. Our decades of marriage, it's all been for this. For the two of us, so we can be who we are now. And you're telling me—what? That's not *us* anymore?"

Mrs. Van Slyke chokes something out and Peety hunches over the table, bringing both fists down. He does it again, and again, tipping over the remaining wine glass. Wine seeps like blood through the tablecloth.

"*Forty years,* Marianne. *Forty years,* and *this* is what it's come to? Spaghetti"—he throws his hand across the table, as if to prove a point—"and a breakup like we're seventeen. I'm *tired*." He pounds his fists on the table, then brings his hands up, shaking his finger in anger. "Everything I've ever done, everything I have *ever done* since I was *twenty* years old has been for *us*. It's been for *us*, Marianne. Do you think this is the life I want? Every day exactly the same, the Mine, then the shop, the kids—not for *me*, for *us*. It's all been for us. *Gahh!*" Peety actually screams, an anguished noise I don't think I've ever heard a living creature make before. Mrs. Van Slyke shrinks into her chair.

"This plate here? We own this plate. This plate is *ours*." He picks up the dish and throws it into the wall—it shatters, the rubbery mass of spaghetti and sauce falling to the floor. He takes the second plate of spaghetti and does the same, further smearing the wall with red and the floor with wreckage. Then he takes the two glasses of water and hurls them to the floor, where they explode in puddles. He turns toward the serving platter in the middle of the table, picks it up, turns it to the side, and slams it against the table, breaking into large fragments with a *kkcrack*. He lets out a wail and slams the fragment he was still holding back into the pile, stabbing the pile of spaghetti and ceramic, again and again, screaming, until his hands are dripping with sauce and blood.

"*Is this all we are to you?*" he yells, picking up the bottle of wine. I stand there, frozen, as Mrs. Van Slyke looks up at him in sheer terror. Paper-white and with eyes like saucers, she cowers in the chair.

He's going to kill her, I think numbly.

He raises the wine bottle as if to strike, his face a mask of anger and anguish, every muscle in his body tensed. He holds it there for a second that feels like eternity before bringing the bottle down.

It strikes the table, holding its form. Peety grabs the bottle by its neck and brings it against the table again, and again, and again, yelling like an animal in pain. Wine *glub-glubs* onto the table and the floor, droplets splattering on the walls and the ceiling. Even when the liquid stops flowing, he keeps pounding and pounding and pounding, denting the table and yelling until the bottle finally cracks and shatters.

Only then does the shouting stop. Peety stands there silently in a wreckage of spaghetti and wine, ceramic and glass shards, heaving.

A few long seconds pass before I realize I'm holding my breath. I let it out as a similar spell seems to break inside the house. Mrs. Van Slyke unfolds unsteadily from the chair and stands in the midst of the mess.

Peety says something in a small voice I can't catch. Mrs. Van Slyke totters unsteadily away from the table, and he goes to catch her wrist.

"Marianne, I'm sorry, I'm so sorry. I don't know what to do, how to *feel*—" Peety chokes on his own words. Mrs. Van Slyke goes to walk away from him, but he holds fast, pulling her toward him instead.

It all happens quickly.

Peety pulls on her arm as she steps back onto some pooled liquid, a shard of plate or of glass, something—and she slips, catching her head on the edge of the table.

"*Marianne!*" Peety screams, not for the first time tonight but for the first time like *this*. Through the window, I can see her limp form, sprawled in a puddle of liquid mixing on the floor. I can't tell what is sauce, what is water, what is wine, and what might be blood.

Peety scrambles to her side. Lifting her limp head to his lap, he screams again, breaking me from the reverie I've fallen into. I run for the front door, but my legs aren't working right, *nothing* is working right. I lunge up the front steps, trying the handle, trying it again, but it's locked. *Back door,* I think. Mind all scrambled and blank and scared, I fall down the front steps and run to the back of the house. Numb, limbs blunt and heavy, I slam open the door. I'm in their kitchen, I hear the wailing, I come around the corner where Peety is hunched over Mrs. Van Slyke.

"Marianne, Marianne, Marianne," he keeps saying over and over and over. I can't tell if she's dead or unconscious, but she lies in a pool of red, and Peety has blood on his hands. I don't know where it's from.

I can't think, can't feel, I'm all broken everywhere. I take a step forward and crunch on a shard of glass. Peety looks up at me, uncomprehending, as if asking why I'm here, in his home.

"Sam?" He looks down at his wife. "Marianne . . ." He looks towards me, not able to meet my eyes. "Help her. Please." Something in me falls into place, at least for a second.

It's all a blur. I slam out the back door and I'm at a neighbor's, ringing their doorbell again and again and again until a light comes on. It takes forever, forever, we don't *have* forever, until a man opens the door.

"It's the middle of the night, kid—" he starts, but stops when he sees me. "What's going on?" he asks, concerned.

"Phone," I stammer. "I need a phone. There's been—an, an accident. Someone's been hurt." He opens the door and leads me to where a landline sits on an end table. I grab it up and dial 911 with shaking fingers.

"911, what's the address of the emergency?"

"Uh, I don't know . . ."

"Does someone else know? Is there someone else there who would know the address?"

I mutely hand the phone to the man, hands shaking, who rattles off a street and a house number. "Some kid came knocking on my door, says there's been an emergency and someone's hurt. I don't know." He takes the phone from his ear. "They want to talk to you again."

"Can you tell me the nature of the accident?" the operator questions me.

"Someone might be dead . . . a neighbor."

The man's eyes widen. "Which neighbor?"

"Van Slyke. Mrs. Van Slyke." The 911 operator keeps talking to me, but I drop the phone. The man picks it up from the carpet and starts to speak, looking at me, but I don't know what he's saying. I walk into the kitchen and sit on the floor, leaning against the cabinets.

By this point, the man's wife is awake and standing at the foot of the stairs. She must have picked up on fragments of the conversation, because she puts her hand over her mouth in a gesture of horror. She turns the light on in the kitchen and fetches me a cup of water. I sit there, staring, uncomprehending, like my brain has shut down. She puts the water in front of me. I look at it blankly. All I can picture is the shattered glass on the floor. Wine on the table. Crumpled metal. Blood on the hands.

Finally, she takes my palm and places the cup of water in it, wrapping my fingers around it in a tight grip. I'm shaking violently; water splashes from the lip of the cup and onto the linoleum. Suddenly, there's more water on the floor. A puddle. I think I've dropped the cup.

———————

The rest of the night passes in a blur. It can't have been more than twenty minutes since I left the house, but it feels like eternity. Or maybe it feels like a blink, I don't know. Nothing makes sense.

Emergency lights flash somewhere and eventually someone comes and collects me, handing me a blanket. I'm shivering but I'm not cold. Another person checks my health. Then I'm in the back of a squad car with an officer I must know. *Officer McLerny*, some voice deep inside me says. He drops me off at home, opening the door and ushering me inside, where Mom is waiting for me anxiously.

"Your husband picked a hell of a weekend to take off, ma'am." Mom's face is a sheet of white.

She puts me into bed. I look at the clock; it's 11:38. Mom keeps talking to me, and I keep staring at the lit display. *11:47. 11:52. Bad duck*, I think. Mom is still here, asking me if I need anything. I don't respond. All I see is blood, blood. Glass, metal, and blood. *11:59, bad duck, bad duck.*

I close my eyes. It's almost time.

FRIDAY

It's 6:58 in the morning, and my eyes open like clockwork. I lie there for a second, staring at the ceiling. I think I'm going to puke, but I don't.

I can't stop seeing Mrs. Van Slyke, lying there in Peety's lap. *It's not real,* I think. *It didn't happen, not really.* It's Friday, and the things that happened—the things that Peety *did*—are either in a past that never existed or a future that will never come to pass. But that reality doesn't make me any less nauseous.

By the time I roll out of bed, it's 7:15 a.m. I grab a pair of jeans and a T-shirt, brushing my teeth in the bathroom. I notice the shirt is inside out, so I fix it. I look terrible, but that's all right. I feel terrible.

I stumble downstairs, where Mom is sitting at the table and sorting through some papers. "You're going to be late," she says. I grunt, and she frowns, peering at me intently. "Are you feeling all right?"

I grunt again, picking my backpack off the couch. I head out the door, get my bike, and pedal off.

Mom was right—I am late. My watch tells me it's 7:27

a.m., and school starts at 7:45. I can't bring myself to care. I still have things I need to get done this morning.

Like every morning, the sun is up and it's humid. I shouldn't have worn a gray shirt; I'm going to sweat through it. The wind whips through my hair as I pedal and pedal downtown, trying to keep my mind off things, to focus on the heat and the air and not on the pit in my stomach that feels wide enough to swallow me. *It doesn't matter,* I tell myself. *It didn't happen. It doesn't matter. Don't think about it.*

I drop my bike in front of the library. As it clatters against the pavement, I sprint over to the hedges, where I let out a low whistle.

"Here, boy. Where are you, Baxter?" I peer into the growth and see fur, so I stick my arms in and fish about until I make contact, pulling out a very dirty white dog.

"Come on, boy," I say, cradling him in my arms as I pick up my bike. "Let's get you home." I look at my watch—already past seven forty. I run my fingers through my hair, thinking. *If I go south, I could shave off some time. It might be faster.* As a rule, I try not to shake things up on the fly, but today has already been a wash. I don't think about why that is. If I go south to get to Mrs. Dean's, there's a park I can cut through. It'll be tough on the bike, but it might be worth it to save the time.

I look at Baxter. "We're going south, buddy." He looks back at me blankly and tries to lick my nose, an attempt I deftly dodge. "No time for that today," I admonish him. "We're already late."

Cradling Baxter, I ride south. Downtown is sleepy this time of day, when the shops haven't opened yet. It never truly gets busy, anyway, no matter the time of day or the day of the week. Occasionally, a lonely car filters by. I still don't feel well, but I'm trying to shake it off when last night's events bubble to the top. *It's not real,* I tell myself as I pedal. *Not really.* But this reassurance only helps so much. I still see Peety when I close my eyes.

Bad duck, the voice whispers. *You did this. Bad duck.*

I think I'm going to crack. I don't want to go to school. I don't want to bring Baxter home. I don't want to be outside at all today; I want to curl up in bed and stay there forever. But I have things to do, and I'm doing them. So I shove all those emotions deep, deep down and bike toward the park.

"Park" is a big word for what this is; it's more of a wooded area that lines the southern border of downtown on the west side of the street. It's not very large, probably only a block by a couple blocks, but the woods are thick, and the path is crap for bikes. Still, I push on.

The path opens to the road and I steer toward it, making my way into the park. It's made of hard-packed dirt, but it's rocky and hard to navigate with one hand. Baxter sees a squirrel and starts yipping at it. I think I'm going to drop either him or the bike, but I don't.

I'm almost out of the woods, literally and figuratively, when a tree root comes out of nowhere and catches my front tire. I'm not going fast enough for it to do any real damage, but it knocks me off balance and makes me tip over my bike. In a flash, Baxter wriggles out of my arm, intent on exploring.

"Hey, Baxter! Come here, boy!" I call to him, quickly picking up myself and the bike. He looks at me and trots further away. "Come on, Baxter," I beg. "We do *not* have time for this." Every time I get closer to him, he moves further away. "Baxter. Come here," I call sternly, but with no effect.

Just then, I see a squirrel out of the corner of my eye. He sees it too. *Crap,* I think, and with that he's off, a little white flash running across the road. I push my bike through the rest of the woods and hop on, pedaling after him.

"Come, Baxter, come!" I shout, but it's useless. The squirrel scampers a few houses down, but by the time Baxter gets there it's nowhere to be found. I think he might come to me now, but no, he's had a taste of freedom again and is not interested in me or my pleading. He's running through yards, stopping every so often to yip back at me excitedly.

He crosses the street in front of me and sniffs at a long line of hydrangeas. This yard is mostly fenced, and I'm able to corner him between some tulips by the front of the house. "Come on, Baxter," I coax. "Aren't you ready to go home?" He looks at me with his blank eyes. I go to scoop him up, but he does that evasive maneuver dogs do when they're playing.

"Baxter, I am *so* late for school." He goes to duck away, but I'm able to catch him just in time. I rest in the yard for a second, picking him up and holding him to my face. "You're an old dog. Who knew you still had some moves in you, huh?" He tries to lick my nose again. This time, I let him.

Hauling myself back on my bike, I pedal for Mrs. Dean's. I look down at the little dog, who isn't struggling as much as he normally does. "Does Mrs. Dean not walk you enough? Is that it?" I ask, but Baxter doesn't answer.

I pull up in front of her house, knocking on the front door. When she answers, she looks at me questioningly.

"Hello, Sam. I wasn't expecting to see you, especially this early in the morning." She sees Baxter and exclaims, "Baxter! Did he get out?" Pulling the screen door open, she takes him into her arms.

"Yeah, I found him by the library. He really gave me a run for my money this time."

"This time?" Mrs. Dean looks at me quizzically.

"Oh, I just meant—he gave me a chase, that's all."

"You know what he likes? Cheese. My Baxy-boo is a little cheese lover. If you have some cheese, he'll come right to you," she explains, in the tangential way all old ladies seem to talk. Then, she screws up her nose. "You need a bath, Baxy." She looks back at me. "Thank you so much for bringing him home. You're a dear."

I smile politely. "No problem at all. I'm late for school; I've got to get going. See you, Mrs. Dean."

She waves to me as I pedal northeast, but I still have one last stop to make.

I coast to a stop in front of a house that no longer has a newspaper at the bottom of the driveway, then drop my bike on the street and run up the drive. I'm sure I'm a mess already—I have dirt on my clothes from the dog chase, I've sweated through my shirt, my hair is a mop, and I probably smell. Still, I knock on the door.

A long moment later, a lady in her forties with thinly rimmed glasses and a jean jacket greets me warily. "Good morning," I tell her. I haven't thought of what to say after this, so I let the words rush out. "I don't think we know each other, but I wanted to ask you if you've talked to Chrissy about what she's doing tonight?"

The lady looks at me blankly. "I'm . . . sorry," she says slowly. "I don't follow."

"Well, you should ask her about it. Talk to Chrissy, ask her what she's doing tonight. You'll want to know, I promise," I say, backing off the porch. "You have a good day," I shout as I pedal off.

"Sorry, who are you?" the lady yells down the street, but I just wave.

———————

Pedaling north, I drop my bike at the bike rack in front of the school. I catch my reflection in the glass double doors at the front of the school and sigh. I was right—I am a mess.

I stop by the front desk, where Vanna is peering at a computer screen from behind thick glasses. She looks up as I walk over. "Good morning, dear. Tardy, are we?"

"I found a lost dog," I explain.

Nodding wisely, she replies, "If that's true, it's quite admirable. If it's a lie, it's more imaginative than the excuses I usually hear." She passes me a clipboard with a sheet attached. "Fill this out and head to class."

I do so. The hallways are still and quiet, which is a change from how I usually experience them. I tap my fingers restlessly against my leg. It's been a long day already.

As I push open the door to my first class, the substitute teacher looks up at me. "Hi," I introduce myself. "Sam Riley. I'm tardy."

"Okay," she says. "We've got a full class today, then. Sit, please."

A *full class today*? I think, confused.

My eyes find the usually empty seat, the one two rows up from mine, the one that today is occupied by—

Ashley Albert, I realize with a start. This is the first time she's been to school in . . . *forever*, I think. *The first time in forever.*

My mind starts to race. *Why today? Why this Friday? Is it something I did? Why—*

"Sam?" the substitute says impatiently. I realize I've been standing in the doorway, staring at Ashley while she scribbles intently on her worksheet.

"Sorry," I mumble, and slide into my desk.

I drop my bag to the floor and listen to the drone of the substitute. I do the worksheet and the time passes. I've done this lesson countless times before, and finish with it quickly today. All the while, that question still burns. *Why today? Why today?*

A couple more classes pass, and it's lunchtime. I'm not hungry. Between the events of last night, this morning, and Ashley's appearance, there's a low-lying queasiness in my stomach I can't shake. The thought of eating makes me sick.

In the parking lot, I pull out my ham sandwich and find the injured bird helplessly hopping in the grass.

"Yeah, buddy. I'm right there with you," I tell it with a sigh. I pull off a piece of crust and toss it near the bird, who shows no interest. "Still not good enough for you, huh?"

It's a rhetorical question. The bird doesn't answer, doesn't look at me at all. I go inside to fetch Vanna, who is reviewing papers at her desk. "Vanna, I found an injured bird outside."

She looks up at me, concerned. "Oh, the poor thing. We'd better go take a look."

Once we find it, she spends a few moments gazing down at it. "How sad," she says, "to spend your whole life in the sky, only to end up like this." Bending down, she tells the creature, "Don't you worry, we'll get you fixed right up." Looking up at me, she asks, "Will you stay with it? I'll go inside and make a phone call, see if we can't find someone to help our poor little friend here."

I sit with the bird and pick at my sandwich as Vanna heads into the building. I watch it hop, hop, here and there. "You confused, buddy?"

It doesn't react. "I'm sorry you're hurt. Now you're stuck down here, slumming it in the muck with the rest of us." I toss it another piece of crust, which it again ignores.

Eventually, Vanna returns. "You can head inside now, Sam. I called the police station. They're going to send someone out to collect our feathered friend."

"Okay. Thanks, Vanna. Hey, what do you think they do with birds like this?"

"I'm not sure," she says, looking at the hobbled creature. "Give it a tiny little splint, maybe."

I look down at the bird. "Yeah. Maybe."

I head back inside. I'm still shook up about Peety, but the chase with Baxter this morning and now the bird have helped a lot. I'm also still confused about Ashley, but at least I don't feel like I'm going to crack anymore.

———————

The rest of the day passes. In English, Mr. Peters calls his usual question to the class. "Can anyone tell us why, although he's throwing rocks at Henry, Roger chooses to not actually hit him with any of the rocks?"

I'm expecting the usual moment of disinterested silence from the class. Instead, Ashley answers quietly.

"He's under the influence of his previous life. Roger, even far away from the threat of any real consequences, can't bring himself to commit this 'taboo.'"

Mr. Peters nods once, impressed. "That's correct," he says, and moves on.

Finally, the bell rings, and the class filters out. I watch Ashley as she leaves, but I don't move yet. Pretending to look for something in my backpack, I sit at my desk for a long minute as the rest of the classroom empties. Mr. Peters catches my eye. "You need something, Sam?"

"No, I—" my voice falters. I usually don't go to the Big6 after school, but today I feel that I need to. I just don't know if

I can. "I'm trying to remember where I'm supposed to go this afternoon."

Mr. Peters nods. "I do the same thing sometimes. Speaking of remembering, yesterday was your birthday, wasn't it? We have a calendar with all our students' birthdays. I'm sorry I missed it."

"That's okay. I didn't do much for it, anyway."

"Really?" he says, surprised. "That's too bad. Eighteen years is a big milestone."

"Yeah," I say with a sigh. "Everyone keeps telling me that. Well, have a good afternoon."

I turn and make my way outside, where I know Shanna will be waiting for me. Sure enough, she's standing by my bike as I walk over. This part is never not awkward.

"Hi, Shanna," I say.

"Hey, Sam," she greets me back. "I . . . haven't seen you in a while. I wanted to check in."

"Sure. Well, I'm still here."

"Yeah, I can see that." There's an awkward pause before she starts again. "I want to make sure you're doing okay. I don't see you a lot anymore, and I'm worried about you. We haven't talked in a while, and I know things have been hard for you since—"

I cut her off. "Thanks, Shanna. That's nice of you. I appreciate you checking in, but I'm doing okay."

"You're sure you're not just saying that?" she asks.

Awkwardly shouldering my backpack, I echo, "I'm sure I'm not just saying that."

"Okay," she says, stepping back. "Well, if that ever changes, or if you ever want to talk, I'm here for you."

"Okay," I tell her. "Thanks."

"I'm not just saying it, Sam. I really mean it."

I nod quickly. "I know you mean it. I know you do."

At that, Shanna looks at me, satisfied. She seems like she wants to say something else, but she doesn't. Instead, she steps back and moves to leave. "All right. I'll see you later, then?" She says it like a question.

"Yeah, okay," I tell her, and put my hand up in a goodbye. I watch her back as she retreats, her short hair swishing. *I miss her, a little,* I think, looking at my hands, still dirty from this morning.

———————

I pedal into town for my usual four-thirty appointment, trying not to think about what I'm going to do afterward, where I need to go. As I lean my bike against the side of the store, I look at the sun blaring unabashedly up above. *Would it kill you to have one cloud?* I think. I used to love the summer, but now I'm sick of it.

I stand there waiting as people pass me on the sidewalk. I'm so engrossed in not thinking about anything that I almost miss the kid. But then I see a boy, *the* boy, walk in front of me, and I come to.

"Hey!" I yell at him. He turns around, eyes wide. "Put that back."

He freezes in fear for a moment. I step toward him, and he turns around, darting away down the sidewalk like a jackrabbit.

Running my fingers through my hair, I sigh. *Crap, I hate when that happens.*

I push the door open, walking into the store. No one is behind the counter, so I fish the five-dollar bill from my wallet and place it in front of the register.

I fidget anxiously as I get back on my bike. It's time. I can feel the pit in my stomach opening again, the one that closed a little throughout the distractions of the day. I don't want to go back to Peety's, but I know I have to. I have to see for myself that he's okay—that *everything* is okay. I need to make sure.

So, I pedal off toward the Big6. A knot has formed in my stomach, and I feel like I might be sick for real this time, throwing up on the hot asphalt by the side of the road. When I come upon my destination, I lean my bike against the front of the building and take a deep breath to steel myself. It doesn't help at all.

Okay, Sam, I think, psyching myself up before I head in. *How many times have you done this? And last cycle was the first time* that's *happened.* I try not to think about exactly what "that" is. *It was an accident. A mistake, a fluke. And now it didn't happen. It's fine. Everything is fine.* The part about it being a fluke isn't a lie. What happened last night was the first thing of its kind that I've seen.

Is it? the dark little voice says to me.

I shove the voice deep down, ignoring it. Okay, once, when I was bringing home Ryan, the lost boy, he tripped and broke his leg. He started running and his foot got caught, sending him sprawling to the ground, screaming. But there was no way I could have known *this* would happen. That Peety would do *this*.

I push the door of the Big6 open, the bell tinkling, and Peety flashes me a smile before continuing to ring up a man at the register. I wait off to the side for him to finish. Once the man leaves, I approach the counter. "Hey, Peety," I manage. "How's it going?"

Peety looks at me, his smile sliding into a look of concern. "You feeling all right there, Sam? You don't look well. Can I get you some water or something? You're pale."

I smile thinly. "Oh, uh, a long day at school."

Peety nods wisely. "Well, enjoy it. Just wait for adulthood, because it only gets worse from here."

"That's your uplifting advice?"

"Hey now." He shrugs defensively. "Everyone learns it someday. I'm only making sure you're prepared."

"Speaking of adulthood, how have you been these days?"

Peety looks surprised by the question, and I can't blame him. It wasn't my smoothest opening, but I'm nervous and the words coming out of my mouth aren't what I want them to be.

"Things have been well," he says. "I've been well. Most stuff is the same old, same old. Nothing around here much ever changes, but you already know that." Peety puts his hands in his pocket, thinking. "The weather's been hot this year already, though it's even not summer yet, not really. Hmm. What else?" He considers it. "Things with the missus have been good, I think. It's hard to tell. Sometimes, when you spend so much time with someone, you get blind to things. I hope—"

No, no, no. Stop, stop, stop. My stomach drops and I feel my face flush, anxious. This is the opposite of where I wanted this conversation to go. I cut him off mid-sentence. "Actually, Peety, I have something I want to ask you."

Peety stops talking, raising an eyebrow and leaning against the counter. "And what's that?"

I clear my throat, stalling for time. I don't have anything I want to ask him, anything at all—I didn't think this far ahead. Finally I say the first thing that comes to mind: "You, uh, got any cool stories? About the Mine?"

Peety looks confused, then grins. This was a good distraction—he loves talking about the Mine, but he usually tries not to. He knows I think it's boring. "You never want to hear my stories! What's changed?"

"I was thinking about it while I was biking over here. Thought I'd ask," I say.

Peety scratches his nose, considering. "Well, there was the one time the dead man came to work—"

"*What?*" I ask, surprised into actual investment.

"This was a long time ago now, even before I started. So, I didn't see it myself, but I had a couple buddies swear they saw it." Peety gives a heavy sigh. "Well, they say some fellow on second shift came in late one night. Now, this man lived alone. He was normally the real excitable type, but he didn't talk much that day. They asked him where he'd been, but he didn't say anything. Just got right down to work. He went in one tunnel and never came out." Shrugging, he continues, "Folks thought that was strange, but they assumed they must've missed him. They didn't see him at all that rest of the night."

Here, Peety leans toward me intently, his voice turning to a whisper. "The next day, the foremen gathered all the miners together and told them he'd died the night before. Heart attack, right there at his kitchen table. Body was found that morning. Dead already, he would've been then, when my friends saw him at work."

"Wow," I say, marveling. "How have I heard so many of your stories, but I've never heard that one before?"

A mischievous smile forms on his face. "Well, that's because I made it up."

I return his grin. "You got me. Still, strange things happen here all the time. A dead man coming to work wouldn't be the weirdest, I guess. You ever see anything else weird like that?"

"Oh, strange things used to happen in the Mine all the time. Why're you asking, Sam? Something going on that I should know about?"

"Nothing like that. I'm just curious."

Maybe he can sense I'm lying. For a while, all he does is stare at me; then he rubs the bridge of his nose, suddenly exhausted. "Sam. I've known you since you were a tyke. These last few months have been hard on you, and I want you to know that I'm here if you need anything. That people still care about you."

I shift uncomfortably, but before I can answer, the doorbell chimes. I look over to see—

Ashley Albert, I think with a start.

For the second time today, here she is. She has a backpack slung over one shoulder and her hand in her pocket. From the corner of my eye, I see Peety looking at me, and I realize I'm staring at her.

As I hastily I break my gaze, Peety gives me a funny look. "Well, if you ever need anything, anything at all, you know where to find me," he says with a small frown.

I nod my thanks, and Peety tactfully drops the topic now that someone else is within earshot. "You see the weather this weekend? Sheesh. It's like living in a barbecue," he says.

Forcing a smile, I reply, "Yeah. And we don't even have the food to show for it."

Peety snaps his fingers, like he just remembered something.

"Sam, wasn't yesterday your birthday? Your ma came in for gas and mentioned it. Why didn't you say anything?"

I shrug. "I just didn't."

"Eighteen years. My eighteenth birthday feels like forever ago. Boys' eighteenth birthdays used to be a big deal in this town. Coming of age, and all." I mentally prepare myself for another birthday speech, which I feel like I've heard a thousand times already.

Instead, we're interrupted. Ashley Albert has finished making her lazy lap around the store and is walking up to the counter. As she points at the jar of Slim Jims sitting by the register, I try not to stare. "How many can I buy for fifteen dollars?" she asks.

Peety looks surprised. "Seven, I figure," he says after doing the mental math.

Nodding, Ashley hands over a wad of crumpled bills. "Seven, please."

Peety hands her the Slim Jims and a few coins for change. She shoves the snack sticks into her backpack, which is already overpacked to the point that she has a hard time working the zipper closed. "Thank you," she says, and turns to head out. Peety and I watch her as she leaves.

"Well, there's a girl that must really love her Slim Jims," Peety observes dryly. "You know her?"

"Uh, just from school," I say as I check my watch. It's getting late and I'm getting hungry. I tell Peety as much.

"Well, you're welcome to help yourself to something, if you'd like. Free snack for the birthday boy."

"Oh, yeah? Is that a rule?"

"Sure is. It's in the Big6 bylaws."

I shake my head anyway. It's been a long day, and I'm still not quite over what happened last night. "Thanks, but I've got to head out."

———————

Standing outside, I quickly scan the area. I can't help it. I want to see Ashley, want to know why she's here. I can't exactly *ask* her why, but I can—I don't know what. Do something, maybe. Anything.

No luck, though—she's not in the parking lot, or down the road. So, I pick up my bike and start to pedal off. Then, something fluttering in a tree catches my attention. Dropping my bike and walking closer to it, I can see that it's an empty Slim Jim wrapper that's been tied to a branch.

It's by a path that's been cut into the woods. I think the path leads to an old fire trail, but there's nothing in the woods over that way, so I never use it. Pulling the wrapper off the tree, I stick it in my pocket, then walk my bike into the woods a little way and drop it to the scrub. There's a fork in the road, to the left or to the right; I take off to the right, unsure of what I'll find.

A few hundred feet along the path, I see a girl sitting in a tree. She's chewing on something—a Slim Jim, probably. Her right leg dangles off the branch, swinging as she watches me. Her face is expressionless; she reminds me of a cat perched on a windowsill, surveying the world outside. I walk closer. "I think you dropped something."

She looks down at me blandly but doesn't respond. When I pull the wrapper out of my pocket and hold it up, she simply says, "I didn't drop that."

I shrug. "'You dropped this' sounds better than 'you littered this.'"

She seems to consider this for a moment. "It does sound better," she agrees.

A long second passes as I slide the wrapper back into my pocket.

"You're Ashley, right?" I ask when it's clear she's not going to say anything else. "We're in class together. Is this how you spend your Fridays? Sitting in trees?"

A shrug. "Not usually," she says mildly. This conversation is going nowhere.

"Well, uh, I wanted to return this to its rightful owner."

"Keep it," she tells me. She takes a newly emptied Slim Jim wrapper, the wrapper from the stick she's just finished eating; then she reaches up and ties it to a branch above her.

"Are you collecting them?" I ask, curious.

"Something like that." She pauses for a second. "I do have five more."

I smile, but she doesn't. I get the feeling she wants me to leave, but I'm not sure I'm ready yet. "I had a second cousin who ate too many Slim Jims. He ended up growing a third arm."

Ashley takes a look at the back of one of the wrappers, reading the ingredients list. "It says here the first ingredient is beef, not uranium. I'll be fine."

"Ah, well. One day you'll wake up with fifteen fingers, and you won't be able to say I didn't warn you," I joke.

She considers that seriously. "Depending on where it grows from, I might not have a problem with a third arm."

"My cousin's arm came right out of the middle of his back. He was a back sleeper, so it gave him a lot of issues."

At that, Ashley gives a small smile, the first I think I've seen from her. "That is a shame. Give your cousin my condolences."

"Will do," I say, but I don't want to let the conversation die out yet. I need this. I need to talk to her. "What do you have in that backpack? *Lord of the Flies*?"

She shrugs. "And other things."

"Looks to me like a lot of other things," I tell her, checking my watch. It's almost six. "It's getting to be kind of late. I know it'll be light out for a while still, but are you heading home? I'll walk you there if you live in town."

"I'm not going home," she says.

"Not going home? As in, not going home right now?" I ask, confused.

"No. I'm staying here tonight."

". . . you're camping?"

"Yes."

"Oh, okay," I say, taken aback. "Well, good thing Slim Jims are nonperishable."

"Good thing," she echoes.

I don't want to leave, but I also don't know how to stay. Not sure what to do, I relinquish the conversation. "Okay. Well, have a nice evening, then. Break a leg, or whatever they say as good luck for camping."

"Don't break a leg, or whatever they say as good luck for riding a bike," she says. I chuckle and give a wave, backing away slowly.

What a weird conversation, I think as I find my bike and pedal off. Like pulling teeth, but . . . I didn't hate it.

For the thousandth time, I wonder why she was in school today. Now, I also wonder why she's camping out in the woods. I think about her backpack. As full as it is, I can't really consider what she seems to be doing "camping." I tell myself it's none of my business, because it isn't. But still, I wonder.

———————

Finally home, I drop my bike by the side of the house. It's almost six thirty, and I'm late for dinner. Mom glances up from the stove, where she's using an old spatula to serve pieces from a rectangular pot pie. She gives an absent "hello" as she cuts, her mind elsewhere.

"How was your day?" she asks, handing me a plate. I take it.

"I don't know," I say offhandedly, as Mom darts me a look of confusion. "I'm tired. It was long."

"Hmm. Aren't they all." I smile at that. She heads to sit at the table, and I follow. "How was school?"

I shrug. "Not much to talk about."

"Well, then. How about weekend plans?"

Considering this, I reply, "I might go to the lake." Mom looks concerned, though she tries to hide it. "Gooseberry Lake," I clarify.

She seems relieved. "That'll be nice. It's supposed to be another hot weekend."

"Yeah. Peety says it's like living in a barbecue."

Mom smiles, but it's thin. I take this chance to look at her, really look at her, in a way I haven't done in a while. She's still young, but she has lines by her eyes and her mouth. I wonder if they're from stress. How many emotions can you have before they etch themselves on your face?

She catches me looking at her. "Do I have something in my hair?" she asks, running a hand through her hair instinctively.

I shake my head. Finished with my dinner, I take my plate to the kitchen and head upstairs.

It's past seven, and I have nothing to do. I didn't lie to Mom earlier; I don't know how my day was. At this moment, I realize exactly how tired I am. Tired and confused. *And lonely*, I think.

Peety. Ashley. So much has happened, and I've had no time to process any of it. I feel like someone has taken me, broken me into pieces, and put me back together a little bit wrong.

I sit on the edge of my bed and rub my eyes. Then I stand, take a shower, and eventually go to sleep.

While I sleep, I dream.

———————

I'm on my bike. I'm not moving. The air is still. The road is a dark, dark, inky nothing, the humidity like a weight and the blackness like a blindfold as I begin to coast, coast through the night, pedaling, pedaling.

I don't know where I'm going. I can't see, can't hear, can only feel the sticky heat of the night.

I start to get anxious. It claws at my stomach. I pedal faster, faster, faster, breathing ragged, muscles straining. It's worse now, turning my guts upside down. Faster still, I pedal, streaming through the air, through the night, breathing wretched, body wracked until I can't take it, still moving, when—

SATURDAY

I wake suddenly, sitting upright in my bed with a start. The feelings begin to fade as my heart rate slows.

Just a dream, I think, as I run my fingers through my hair. Shaking it off, I get out of bed and start the day, pulling on clothes and heading downstairs.

What to do on a Saturday? *More like, what to do on a Saturday that I haven't done already?* I think as I pop slices of bread into the toaster.

My mind turns to Ashley. She didn't seem to want me there, didn't seem to want to talk to anyone, but I have to know what's going on, why she's here. Besides, I've never been one not to let curiosity get the better of me. So, I gather up my $7.75, my backpack, and my swimming trunks, and head off.

When I first go outside, it's merely warm, but it's turning hot already as I bike, and I sweat as I pedal, pedal, pedal northward. It takes over half an hour to get to the Big6 and the path by the woods where I saw Ashley yesterday. Dropping my bike, I walk into the woods, wondering, not for the first time, what exactly it is that I'm doing.

I make my way to the tree from yesterday. Sure enough, I see Ashley sitting on the ground with her back against the trunk. Closing a paperback copy of *Lord of the Flies*, she looks up at me. If she's surprised, she doesn't show it.

"Hey," I say, awkwardly. "Just checking to make sure you weren't eaten by bears or something."

"No bears."

"No third arm either?"

She takes her book and slides a bookmark between the pages in a surprisingly meticulous motion. "No third arm."

"No third arm, *yet*," I tell her. "How many Slim Jims you got left?"

She looks up to an overhanging branch, where I count six Slim Jim wrappers tied in knots in a neat row. "I ate them all."

"I think . . . I think if you were going to grow another arm, it would have happened by now."

"Shame," she says.

I smile and motion toward her book. "*Lord of the Flies*?"

Nodding, she replies, "I'm rereading. It's . . . powerful."

I'm surprised. This is the first time she's volunteered any information—maybe we're starting to get somewhere. "Yeah? Something about living in the wild is really speaking to you?"

This gets me her second small smile. "I hadn't thought about it that way."

Taking a step closer, I ask, "So, how was your night in the woods?"

"Uncomfortable," she says.

"That figures. We invented beds for a reason, I guess." There's an awkward pause. "Have you, uh, had breakfast?" I ask.

She peers up at me curiously. "Have you?"

I think about lying, but decide not to. "Yeah, I had some toast. But, you know, I could really go for a Slim Jim right about now." Internally, I grimace—that was lame, even for me.

If Ashley thinks so too, she gives no sign—just stands and stretches, brushing the mulch and dirt from her legs. "I do like Slim Jims." She picks up her few things, which are scattered about, and puts them in her backpack. It's a ratty canvas thing, drawn on with a pen in certain places and stuffed to the point of bursting.

I try to make small talk as we find our way out of the woods. "Any particular reason you're camping out here?"

Ashley looks at me. "Yes," she says. I give her a moment to explain, but she doesn't elaborate. I think about asking again but decide not to pry.

Peety looks up from the register as I open the door to the Big6—for a second, I think his jaw is going to hit the floor. I walk up to the counter. "Hey, Peety. How's business?"

"Slow. Same as usual. And you must be Ms. Slim Jim?"

Ashley smiles, but doesn't respond.

"You can call her Ashley—Ms. Slim Jim is her mother." I'm taking a chance on the joke; I don't know Ashley well and I don't know if she'll think it's funny.

She tucks a stray strand of hair behind her ear. "He's right. My full name is Ashley Slim Jim."

Relieved, I turn back toward Peety. "That offer of a free snack for the birthday boy still on the table?"

"Sure is. What'll you be having?"

I turn to Ashley, who points at the Slim Jim jar. "One of those, please," I tell Peety.

"Tell you what—I'll even give you two. Eighteen is a special birthday, after all." He fishes a couple sticks from the jar and hands them over the counter. "What're you two up to today?"

I haven't thought that far ahead. "Um, we're just eating breakfast for now."

Peety arches his eyebrow. I can tell he wants to say something, but he doesn't. "All right. Well, you have fun, now. And watch out for the heat, it's supposed to get to almost a hundred."

Promising Peety that we will, I'm about to turn to leave when Ashley pipes up. "Do you have a bathroom?" she asks.

"We sure do, right around that corner." Peety points to the back wall of the Big6, where a short hallway wraps off to the side. Once Ashley is safely around the corner, he turns back to me with a wide smile. "So, a girl, huh?"

I grimace. I should have seen this coming. "It's, uh, not like that. I don't even know her. I mean, she's in my class, but I really only met her yesterday."

Peety doesn't seem to be listening. "You could have picked a better first-date breakfast spot than two Slim Jims at a gas station."

"Peety, you're not doing yourself justice. This isn't just a gas station, it's *the* Big6."

Judging by his expression, he isn't having any of my jokes. "Yeah, yeah," he says, fishing two more Slim Jims out of the container and handing them over the counter.

"Peety, you don't need to give me these," I protest, but he waves me off.

"Take them. For good luck and all that."

"Thanks, Peety. I appreciate it." I stick them in my backpack as Ashley rounds the corner.

We say our goodbyes, then head outside to the lonely picnic table sometimes used by the mechanics on their lunch breaks. Cigarette butts litter the grass, and I brush a couple off the top of the table and onto the ground.

"Hmm. Who's littering now." Ashley says it as a statement, rather than a question.

"Ah, you got me. No one's perfect all the time."

I sit on the bench and she sits on the table, feet resting next to me—not *right* next to me, but a comfortable distance away. I'm suddenly acutely aware of the fact I don't *actually* know what I'm doing at all. It's not like I'm dating this girl, or even want to date this girl, or have thought about that at all, no matter what Peety might say. It's more like—how can you suddenly choose to invite someone into your life? How can you walk up to them and decide they're a person you should spend a day with? *Why am I doing this?* I think, suddenly uncomfortable.

As soon as I think it, the answer is obvious. After the same three days over and over and endlessly over again, this is the first time Ashley Albert has ever come to school on a Friday. I don't know why, or if it's important, or if it's even a *good* thing she finally made it to school, but at least it's different. *If one thing is different, it might mean—it might mean—*

But I don't let myself finish the thought. All I know for sure is it means that today, I'm not alone. And on this scorching Saturday midmorning, sitting on a bench and eating a disgusting meat snack in only semi-awkward silence, that's good enough for me.

I look down at the Slim Jim I opened unconsciously. "You can have the rest of mine, if you want," I say, offering it to Ashley.

"Are you sure?"

"Yeah. I'm not a big Slim Jim fan," I admit.

Shrugging, she reaches out for the stick. "Like you said. No one's perfect all the time." She rips off the piece I bit into last and offers it to me.

I take it from her and throw it into the woods. "For the ants," I tell her.

She nods solemnly. "More littering," she says, and munches contently.

All this time, I've been thinking about how to broach the subject; at last, I decide there's no tactful way to do it. "Do you live in the woods? Full time, I mean."

There's a pause as she swallows. "No. For last night. And maybe tonight, but not forever."

"Ah, okay. That's good, I guess."

Struggling for further words, I'm glad when Ashley speaks instead. "Thank you for the breakfast. I didn't mean to make you use your birthday snack on me. Especially since you don't like Slim Jims."

"Oh, no problem. It's no big deal."

"Birthdays," she says, "are a big deal. Especially your eighteenth. You only get one birthday a year, and one eighteenth birthday in a lifetime. Did you do anything for your birthday?"

I shake my head. "Not really. We ordered pizza and watched a movie. My mom wanted to make a cake, but I thought that was too much, so she brought home cupcakes instead."

Ashley neatly folds the Slim Jim wrapper into quarters, then ties it in a knot, sticking it in her pocket. "Did you get any gifts?"

I think of the pile of opened envelopes from my relatives. Envelopes that I hadn't opened. "I guess." If this is a weird response, Ashley doesn't comment on it. "So, then, what does your family do for birthdays?" I ask her.

"I was grounded over my last birthday."

"Grounded?" I say, surprised. "Why?"

"Do you know the ribbon page markers that are stuck in the spines of hymnals to mark pages during service?" She pantomimes placing a marker and closing a book.

"I think so. I mean, I at least have an idea of what you're talking about."

"I cut them all off."

I don't know what I was expecting her to say, but it sure wasn't that. "You cut the ribbons off all the song books? At your church?" She nods. "That's . . . unusual. You're not the religious type, then?"

She doesn't answer my question. "The ribbons are tied to an insert. I spent my birthday re-tying new ribbons."

"Hmm," I say, not sure how to respond. There's a long moment of silence. "You have any plans for today?" I ask.

Ashley looks at me. "We both know I don't."

"I didn't know if you have to reread *Lord of the Flies*, or take a nap on the ground, or organize your Slim Jim wrapper collection."

"The ground is not that comfortable, and my collection isn't going anywhere," she says.

Smiling, I tell her, "It's going to be a hot day. Want to go to the lake?"

"Stevens Point?"

"No," I say, a little too quickly. "Gooseberry."

She nods slowly. "Have you had a gooseberry?"

I toy with telling her that, until recently, I didn't know gooseberries were a real fruit, but then think better of it. "I don't think so."

"And I've never been to the lake. Okay. Let's go." She stands up and brushes her fingers on her shorts, which are already smudged with dirt.

"All right, then. To the lake it is." Rising, I motion over to my bike.

Ashley frowns. "There's only one seat."

I laugh. "I mean, yeah. It's a bike."

"Where do I sit?"

"You sit on the crossbar," I reply, pointing to the part of the frame that stretches horizontally from beneath the seat to beneath the handlebars.

"You're serious?"

"Totally serious."

Looking concerned, she chews her lip and seems to consider it. "How long have you been riding a bike?"

"For pretty much as long as I can remember."

"Have you crashed your bike?"

At this, I take a hard gulp and swipe at my hair. I think about—about tipping my bike and losing Baxter in the woods.

"Not, uh, recently," I say, not looking at her directly.

"Have you ever ridden with a second person on the bike?" Ashley asks.

I used to ride with Shanna on the crossbar sometimes. She has a bike but doesn't like to use it, preferring to have her friends drive her. In a pinch, though, she'd sit on my crossbar and I'd pedal her into town. Sometimes I'd even take her here to the Big6, where, when she wasn't looking, Peety would wink at me and I'd pretend not to notice. But that was a while ago. "I used to be pretty good. I haven't done it in a while, but I bet it'll come back to me. Just like riding a bike, right?"

I compose myself and shoot Ashley my winningest smile, which she doesn't return, so I drop it. "We could walk, but it'll take us a good couple hours. It'll be a lot faster if we bike."

"Okay," she says, conceding. "Tell me what to do."

I show her how to sit on the crossbar with both her legs thrown to the left side of the bike. She's seated in front of and below me, and I have to wrap my arms around her to grasp the handlebars. I think neither of us is particularly comfortable with the arrangement, but she does her best to be politely ignorant of the fact I'm breathing into the top of her head, and I do my best to keep my elbows bowed out and around so I'm touching her as little as possible. We have a wobbly takeoff, but in no time we're coasting on the shoulder of the road.

"Your family from the area, then?" I ask, and she nods. The wind blows her ponytail into my face, surprising me and making me jerk the bike to one side. Ashley yelps, and I correct it quickly. "Sorry, sorry about that," I tell her. I'm more shaken than I should be.

"It's okay. We're not moving fast enough to get hurt," she says, but I ignore her comment.

"So, your family?" I ask again, changing the subject.

"My mom is local. My dad is from Virginia. He moved here to do management work for the Mine. Now that there's no mine, he works for a publishing company." She looks up at me. "I know what your dad does, so I won't ask you the same question." I feel her gaze on me, but I don't look down. "How is having a police officer for a father?"

My answer is honest, if not sincere. "People used to be worried I was going to tell him where the parties were."

"Hmm," she says. "Did you?"

I vehemently shake my head. "No way, never. I'm not a snitch. Besides, that's a sure way to not get invited back."

She looks out over the front of the bike and at the top of the tree line. "It's a beautiful day."

I laugh. "For you! I'm pedaling in ninety-plus degrees of heat, getting baked like a rotisserie chicken."

Ponytail bobbing up and down as she nods in agreement, Ashley adds, "You don't smell great, either." My face flushes red with embarrassment, and I'm glad she can't see it under the sunburn and the sweat.

"Oh, wait," she continues, "that's me."

I laugh again. "It's probably both of us." At that moment, it feels like a kind of tension has been broken, an ice I didn't realize was there.

We ride in silence for a long minute; then Ashley asks, "How far are we?"

"We're about halfway there."

"Do you go to the lake often?"

"Sure, when it's hot in the summer. But usually, we go to—" I realize what I'm saying and I stop myself. "Well, I go to Gooseberry now." Ashley looks up at me, again reminding me of a cat. Her eyes are wide, knowing, and unblinking, in the way cats' eyes are sometimes.

I keep pedaling as we make small talk. I haven't spoken to Ashley much before this, and I find myself surprised by her personality. She's precise and direct, with a dry streak of humor I wasn't expecting.

As I swerve into the dollar store parking lot, Ashley looks around, wondering why we've stopped. I scoop the tab-less beer off the ground.

"Are you going to drink that?" she asks as we pedal off again.

"Only if you don't want it."

She shakes her head. "No, thank you. I'm not much for parking-lot beverages."

Soon we're to the woods around Gooseberry. I have Ashley hop off—I'm not sure if I'm a strong enough pedaler to get both of us safely through on my bike. I walk the bike on the fire trail as Ashley walks next to me. She seems to be lost in thought. "What're you thinking about?" I ask.

She chews her lip and considers for a second. "A bit of everything. Do you always ask people what's on their mind?"

"Hmm." Now it's my turn to consider the question. "No, because most of the time, I don't care."

Ashley smiles. "That's fair." There's a lull in the conversation. "What do you do with your summer days? Other than talk to girls you find in the woods."

"A lot of this, I guess. Sometimes I go into town. I ride my bike a lot. What does anyone do in this place?"

Shrugging, she replies, "I spend most of my free time at church."

This surprises me. "Doing . . . anything in particular?"

"Chores. Cleaning. Organizing. There's Sunday morning service, Sunday afternoon service, Friday night service, and biweekly church member meetings." She ticks these off on her fingers. "They all have to be prepared for and cleaned up after. My mom is very involved, so I'm very involved."

"Wow," I say. "That sounds like a lot. That much time in church could make you crazy enough to cut some ribbons out of books, for sure." It's a joke, but it doesn't land. Ashley ignores it, and I try another approach. "You have any siblings to help with all that?"

"One sister. She doesn't live here anymore."

I wait for her to elaborate, but she doesn't. "I'm an only child," I volunteer.

Ashley looks at me with her wide cat eyes. "Are you lonely?"

I'm a bit taken aback. "Why would I be lonely?"

She shrugs. "I've heard that being an only child can be lonely."

Thinking for a second, I tell her, "I don't think having siblings has anything to do with whether you're lonely or not."

Ashley nods sagely. "That's true."

We come upon the beach, if it can even be considered that. Ashley sits on one of the logs that line the rocky shoreline as I put the hot beer in the water, hoping soon it'll cool down to lukewarm. "The American Dream," she says, watching me.

"America, land of the free . . . parking-lot beer." I lie on the beach, toes in the water. I think about what happened with Peety, then just as quickly try not to think about it. The last couple days have rattled me, but I'm doing okay with keeping my mind off it.

Ashley walks over, and I look up at her. Blinding sunlight rings her head; she looks like a weird, gothic angel. "Can you skip rocks?" she asks.

"No, I can't," I tell her.

"Hmm. I was hoping you could teach me." She walks into the water. It covers the tops of her feet, then reaches her knees, then up to her waist. I sit and watch.

"You're not getting in?" Even though she's forty feet from the shoreline, she doesn't shout—I have a hard time hearing her. Standing up, I wade to my shins, but I don't go in any farther. She walks back to where I am, frowning. "You said you like the water when it's hot."

"Yeah. To look at."

"You come to the lake to look at the water?"

"Yeah," I tell her, and I point to my beer. "And I put my beer in it."

"And people think *I'm* odd." The comment strikes me as strange, but I don't remark on it. She scans the lake and points to the tiny island. "Have you ever swum out there?"

I nod.

"Uh, yeah. I used to sometimes, when I was a kid."

"I'm not a good swimmer," Ashley says, floating back into the water. I watch her for a bit as she bobs here and there. Even if she's far from the most expressive person I've ever met, she seems to be enjoying herself. I sit on the beach and crack open my beer, which is exactly as mediocre as I remember. A while later, Ashley floats her way back to the shore. Her clothes are soaked as she sits down on the log. "How is it?" she asks me.

"It's everything you'd expect a lukewarm parking-lot beer to be."

Ashley picks a small stick off the shoreline in front of her and starts to break it into pieces. "I've never had a beer before."

Once again, I'm surprised by Ashley Albert. House parties and bonfires on the lake are regular events for the high schoolers of Redford. "Do you want to try it?" I ask.

She smiles humorlessly. "No, thank you. If the Slim Jims don't give me a third arm, that will."

I shrug. "Hey. A third arm might help your swimming."

Smiling for real this time, she concedes, "It can't hurt it."

"So." I put the can on the ground and turn to look at Ashley. "How have you managed to go your whole life never having a beer before?"

ABIGAIL STARK **103**

"There's no alcohol in the house," she says mechanically.

"That's . . . not really what I meant. You've never even had one at a party? Or are you a hard liquor kind of girl?"

Once again, the joke doesn't land. "I've never been to a party. My parents wouldn't let me out of the house for that. Even if they did, I don't know if I'd go."

"Strict parents, huh? I know what that's like."

Nodding, Ashley replies, "It must be difficult to have a dad who's a police officer."

"He's . . . not around much."

"Oh," she says. "I'm sorry."

I shake my head quickly. "Don't be. Really. I'm glad he's not around."

"I think my parents are around too much," she says.

Smiling humorlessly, I reply, "If only we could average them out and get happy-medium parents."

"I don't think that's how averages work."

I throw a pebble into the lake. "You tell me. I'm failing math."

She raises an eyebrow. "You might want to look into that."

"Eh, it's all right. Not like I have much of a future, anyway. English is my only good subject. But I'm glad you were in school Friday to answer Mr. Peters' questions."

"To be honest," she says, "the only reason I was able to go to school on Friday is because of you."

Hearing that, I feel my pulse spike suddenly. I'm not sure what she means.

"I wasn't supposed to be in school," she continues. "I'm grounded again. Yesterday morning, when you were in our yard chasing that dog, my parents were watching you long enough for me to grab my backpack and some clothes. I left through the side door. I went to school because I didn't know where else to go."

My stomach drops, and I feel myself go numb. I thought there might be some hope—hope that something has changed, that Ashley being here means something is different this time. But no. It's the same web, same cycle it's always been.

Stupid, stupid, Sam, I think, looking away. *Bad duck.*

It takes everything in me not to scream, not to pound my hands into the sand. Instead, I squeeze the beer so hard I crush the can. I look out at the lake and try to keep it together.

There's a beat of silence. I can tell Ashley is uncomfortable. I don't know if it's because what I did, or what I didn't do. I take a deep breath. I'm not sure what to say.

"Wow. Chasing that dog was a mess, but I'm glad something good came of it." As far as responses go, it's pretty pitiful, but it's all I've got, so it'll have to be enough.

Just to do something, I go back to sipping the beer. I see Ashley watching me, so I hold the can out. "You sure you don't want any?"

She chews on her lip for a moment, then extends her arm. I pass the collapsed can over gently and she sniffs it, making a face. Tentatively, she takes a swallow, then immediately gags. I think more liquid ends up on her shirt than down her throat.

"That's terrible," she chokes out.

I try not to laugh. "If you can eat, like, fourteen Slim Jims, one gulp of lukewarm beer won't kill you."

Wiping her mouth with the back of her hand, she struggles for words. "It tastes like—stale carbonated bagels, but disgusting." I pass her my bottle of water, and she takes a swig. "Why do people drink that?"

Sighing, I stretch out on the beach and let the water lap my toes. "Nothing better to do, I guess. How else are teenagers supposed to pass the time around here?"

Ashley considers this. "Is it fun?" she asks.

"You mean, is drinking fun? I mean, sure. It's fun. It's social. You see your friends, you let loose. You meet new people." Ashley grunts, noncommittal. "What? You have something against fun?"

"I'm not great at meeting new people," she says.

I look out at the lake. "Oh, yeah? Maybe you haven't been given the right opportunity. Either way, that's too bad." There's a long beat. "If you're not a people-meeter, what do you do for fun?" I ask.

"Church, mostly."

"Oh, come on. I said for fun, not because your parents make you."

She chews her lip again before responding.

"I like to write."

"Writing? That's cool. Anything in particular?"

"Poetry. I'm going to be a poet," she says, and I think I believe her.

"That's great. You ever let people read what you write?"

"Some people, sometimes."

"Some people, like me?" I ask.

Ashley smiles. "Unlikely."

I squint into the piercing, blue, seamless summer sky. The heat bakes down on me. I feel like I'm melting into the shore, but it's not unpleasant. "You were right. It is a beautiful day," I say absently.

We spend some time like this, me lying on the shore, her sitting on the log, talking about this and that and working on our sunburns. We don't talk about anything important but all the little things. How we broke bones as kids, what kind of ice cream we like. "Strawberry," Ashley says.

I screw up my nose. "I think you're the first person I've met whose favorite ice cream is strawberry."

"It's underrated. Which means there's more for me."

"Yeah? Well, I like vanilla," I tell her.

"Classic, but plain," she observes.

"I used to like chocolate, but at my tenth birthday party, I ate so much I threw it up." Ashley smiles.

We chat for a while longer. We don't talk about our families. I don't talk about why I'm a loner in a world full of people. She doesn't talk about why she's sleeping in the woods.

Finally, we're hot and tired and ready for something else. I press my palm to my arm and it does the sunburn thing, where the skin turns white and then flushes red. "I could make a lobster jealous."

"We should have brought some sunscreen," Ashley says. I look at her face, which is a bright shade of fire truck.

With a shrug, I check my watch. "Hindsight is twenty-twenty. It's past one o'clock. What're you feeling?"

"I'd like to eat something. I'm hungry."

"I've got less than ten dollars on me," I confess.

Ashley rummages around in her pockets. "I have . . . a quarter and four cents."

"I hate to be a downer, but I don't think this is going to be enough for lunch. If you want, we can eat at my house. My mom is going grocery shopping today, but we could probably still find something."

Ashley considers this, then smiles. "I have a better idea."

———————

Not even ten minutes later, we're back on the bike and I'm pedaling north. The ride is uncomfortable and maneuvering the both of us is difficult, but now that we've spent the morning together, at least it's not awkward.

"Are you sure you want to do this? I don't want you getting caught," I tell Ashley.

"I want to do it," she says softly. She seems distracted, and the breeze almost rips the words away before I can catch them. "What about you? Will you be okay?"

I consider her question for a moment. "The word *consequence* doesn't mean anything to me anymore."

"You might be a bit of a poet yourself, Sam Riley," Ashley says with a smile.

We soon roll into her neighborhood, stopping around the corner from her house. "Drop me here," Ashley instructs, and I do. She hops off the bike. "Do you remember the plan?"

Nodding, I reply, "I ring the doorbell. I tell them I think my dog ran under the deck in the backyard, and I ask if it's all right with them if I try to get him out. You use the side door to get in and out of the house. I pretend to be surprised when my dog isn't there. Then I apologize and leave."

"Good. It should take me less than five minutes."

"I'll see you soon, then." Hopping on my bike, I pedal around the corner. I'm not looking forward to this—I'm not a great actor. *I don't have to be great. I only have to be good enough,* I think to myself.

Bad duck, a different voice mocks. *This is theft.*

I ignore it as I drop my bike on the lawn, running up the steps to the front door, where I ring the doorbell three times in quick succession. Anxious, I run my fingers through my hair.

The door opens a few long moments later. In front of me stands Mrs. Albert, Ashley's mom, a middle-aged lady in thick spectacles and a matronly floor-length denim dress.

"Can I help you?" she asks. Her voice is clipped, and her face is drawn and tired.

"Hi, yeah—I think my dog ran under your deck, and I was wondering if it's okay if I could try to get him out? I don't want you to see me in your backyard and wonder what I'm doing." Letting out a nervous chuckle, I try to give a smile.

"You're the boy from yesterday, aren't you?"

"Oh, ha, yeah. That's me. The . . . repeat offender," I finish awkwardly.

"You should keep that dog on a leash," she says.

I let out another anxious chuckle. "You really think I'd learn, wouldn't you?"

"I would." She starts to come out of the house, but without her husband.

Thinking quickly, I ask, "Do you think we might need a flashlight?"

Mrs. Albert frowns. "It's the middle of the day."

"Just, you know . . . in case?"

Sighing, she relents, "I'll have my husband get one." She leans into the house and yells. "Richard? Can you please get the flashlight, the big one from the shed?"

I hear the sound of someone walking down the stairs, and a man appears in the doorway. "It's the boy from yesterday," Mrs. Albert says. "His dog is loose again. He thinks it might be under the deck."

The man, Ashley's dad, is tall and wiry, and when he peers down at me, he seems concerned. "Son, you ought to take better care of your dog," he tells me.

"You are . . . very right," I say. "And I'm so sorry about this." I motion to the backyard. "Do you mind if I take a look under your deck? Maybe with a flashlight . . . ?" I peter off as they both head outside and into the backyard, with me trailing behind them.

Ashley's dad, Richard, heads into a small, sloping shed as Mrs. Albert walks to the deck. As I lead her to the part of the deck that's furthest from their side door, I wonder if Ashley is okay. I pretend to peer through the lattice that serves as the deck's skirt. Mrs. Albert is talking to herself.

"Two times in two days your dog has come around here. He must like the hydrangeas," she says, motioning to a long line of flowering shrubs. I check my watch. *1:38.* I get down on my knees and peer through the lattice, pretending to search intently for my missing pet.

"Do you see him under there?" she asks.

"I'm not sure yet," I say as I stand and walk around the deck, pretending to find a different vantage point. Richard comes up behind me and hands me a flashlight, a large, boxy thing. It has some weird push-button toggle on it, which I pretend to struggle with. Richard takes it out of my hand, pushes the button, and hands it back.

"Right. Thanks," I say weakly. Getting down on all fours and peering through the lattice, I sweep the light back and forth, stalling for time. *1:40.*

I pretend to see something. "Hey, boy," I call. "Hey . . . Toby." Internally, I grimace. *Where did Toby come from?*

Looking up, I tell the others, "I think I see him." I walk around the deck a bit and pretend to call his name, coaxing my imaginary dog by whistling and snapping my fingers. *1:41,* reads my watch.

Richard frowns. "I thought your dog had a different name? I could have sworn yesterday I heard his name was . . ." He struggles, and then gives up. "Something else," he finishes.

"Yeah . . ." I twist my fingers into the strands of my hair. "His full name is Baxter Toby Riley. I named him when I was a kid. You know how kids are with . . . naming things. Really bad," I finish lamely, and then pretend to be busy with the deck. *1:42.*

I make my way to the stairs and really get in there, straining my arm under the deck and enthusiastically calling to my imaginary dog. "Baxter Toby, here, boy!" I make a whole production of it, even pretending to tweak my shoulder to give me a few seconds of time to wince and roll it.

Finally, my watch reads 1:43, and I feel a flood of relief. I pretend to give up. "I must have seen a rabbit. Whatever it was, it isn't here anymore."

I hand the flashlight back to Richard. "I'm sorry to bother you. I really thought he was under there. I'll, uh, be off then," I say, making a motion toward my bike.

"Shouldn't you leave us a phone number?" Mrs. Albert asks.

I'm taken aback. "For . . . ?"

"For in case your dog comes back. So we can call you."

"Oh! Of course. Yeah, that would be great. That's a great idea, thanks." She fetches a small notepad from inside the house and brings it out to me, along with a pen. Across the top of the notepad is an inspirational Bible quote in flowing script. The pen is from a bank. I jot down my name and phone number and hand them back to the Ashley's mom.

"Good luck finding your dog," Richard calls out as I wave goodbye and pull around the corner on my bike. Ashley stands a couple hundred feet farther along the sidewalk. I coast up to her.

"How'd it go?" I ask.

"I got the money." She looks me up and down. "Somehow, you seem even dirtier than before."

"I spent all morning looking for my lost dog, Toby Baxter. Of course I'm dirty. Will you call me if you see him?" I ask.

Ashley smiles. "Let's get some lunch," she says, sitting on the crossbar of my bike as I take off.

"Toby Baxter!" I call out loudly as we pedal away. "Toby Baxter!" Ashley smacks my leg.

"Someone's going to see me and call my parents," she says. I stop yelling, but I'm grinning like a madman.

———————

Sometime later, we pull into Danny's. It's after two o'clock now, and the place is empty. We slide into a booth in the back of the restaurant. Once again, it feels as hot inside as it does outdoors. When I say this to Ashley, she replies, "At least we're not in the sun."

The waitress saunters over with two large plastic cups of water, which she puts on the table. Her nails are long and red, and they click against the sides of the cups as she sets them down. "My name's Mindy. I'll be your server today." Her voice carries a lilting Southern drawl uncharacteristic of the area. She hands us two sticky, laminated menus and makes her way back to the bar, where she stares at a small box TV on a shelf in the corner. It's playing a grainy courtroom drama.

We both eagerly down the water, and I press the cool plastic cup to my forehead. "What're you having?" I ask. "I always get the burger."

"I don't know yet, I have to look at the menu. I haven't been here before." Once again, Ashley surprises me. "I'll buy," she says.

"In that case, I'll have a burger *and* an extra side of fries."

"I'll have the two-hot-dog weekend special," Ashley says as she sets the menu down.

"You really like hot dogs, huh? Or do you just like the ketchup?" I ask.

She looks at me, surprised. "Both. How did you know?"

"You didn't say something about that earlier?"

"Not that I remember."

"Oh. A good guess, then."

The waitress comes back to take our orders and refill our cups. I eagerly gulp the water, chewing on the ice. "So. Tell me more about the heist," I say as I smoosh the ice around my cup with the straw.

Ashley shrugs. "My dad keeps some money in his office. I . . . helped myself."

I nod solemnly. "Did stealing it bother you?"

Thinking about this, Ashley replies, "I believe that a lot less of what we do matters than we think."

I consider this. "I don't know if I agree with that."

Ashley raises an eyebrow. "What do you mean?"

Crossing my arms, I answer, "There's no way to know what does or doesn't matter. There's no way to know what might change your life."

"Maybe. But if everything we do is important, that means nothing is."

"I don't know. It's tough to say. I think that . . . maybe everything's important, so everything *is* important. Does that make sense? I'm not sure it does," I say, running my fingers through my hair.

"You have a strong opinion on this," Ashley notes.

I realize she's right. "I . . . don't want you to think that nothing matters, because sometimes it's the things you think matter the least that end up mattering the most. And maybe you don't realize it till afterward, and maybe you never realize it at all. What dog you chase, what beach you swim at . . ." *What party you go to,* a tiny voice in my head says. "What girl you meet, you know, what you have for dinner . . ." I trail off, and Ashley nods slowly. "All I mean is—you can't always know what's important in the moment," I say, then pause again. "I don't mean to lecture." Waving my hand, I finish with, "My opinion. Not worth anything."

Ashley takes a long drink of water. "I like your opinion. At least you have one. That's worth something." Putting her cup down, she tells me, "I'm going to make a phone call."

She stands and walks to the counter, where she exchanges words with our waitress. The waitress points at the wall by the kitchen door, where an old, greasy landline is hung. Ashley strolls over to the phone and puts her back to me, leaning against the doorframe as she dials.

Her call is short. She slides back into the booth when she's finished. I want to ask who she was talking to, but I think that's probably bad manners, so I don't. Still, she must see the question on my face.

"I called a friend," she says. I'm surprised, though I couldn't say why. "But I wish I could talk to my sister. She always knows what to do," Ashley continues, chewing on her lip. "I miss her," she adds quietly.

Our waitress comes by to give us the check, but I order another basket of fries instead. I'm not hungry, but I don't want to leave yet.

Staring at the floor, Ashley eventually begins to talk. "Her name is Melissa. She's four years older than I am. I think she's perfect. My parents . . . don't feel that way." She fiddles with her straw uncomfortably. "When we were kids, we'd sit on the back porch and catch fireflies. I had a jar I kept them in. I always let them go at the end of the night, but one night, I forgot. The next day, we had a jar of thirty dead fireflies. I remember the way they sounded." She pantomimes shaking something. "I thought they'd rattle, but they were limp and fat and . . . wet. It was weeks before I could look at a firefly again." She pauses for a second. "Lissa took their bodies and put them in the dirt, where she said they belonged. I would have left them outside in the jar all summer, but she buried them." She pulls a fry from the mound, staring at it as it droops under its own weight.

"She sounds really great," I tell her.

"She is. I call her Lissa. She calls me Ash."

"Those are nice nicknames. It seems like she cares about you," I say sincerely.

"Do you have any nicknames?" Ashley asks.

I'm caught off guard by the sudden change in topic. "Uh, well. My dad calls me Ducky."

"That's a nice nickname too."

I smile humorlessly. "It's not supposed to be. It's short for 'bad duck.'"

Frowning, she says, "I don't know what that means."

"Sometimes my dad will say I'm a bad duck. It's the opposite of a good egg, I think. So, he calls me Ducky, for short."

Ashley nods. "Jerk," she says, making me smile.

"Yeah. Like, you'd think the opposite of a good egg would be a bad egg."

There's silence for a moment before she talks again. "If you have problems with your parents, then I'm in good company." She pushes the plate of fries towards me. "Eat up. You ordered them."

The rest of lunch is more lighthearted. We talk about Ashley's favorite books, none of which I've read. In turn, I tell her about my fifth birthday, which was almost canceled when I was bitten on the butt by a spider so hard I cried and wouldn't come out of the bathroom when guests started to arrive. My party was fire-truck themed, because I wanted to be a firefighter. My dad was always mad I didn't want to be a cop.

"And now what do you want to be when you grow up?" Ashley asks.

"What do you mean? I'm eighteen. I am grown up."

She rolls her eyes. "Not in the 'you're a man now' kind of way this town is obsessed with. If you could do anything. What would you do?"

"I haven't thought about it."

"Never?" she asks, finally her turn to be surprised.

"No, I . . . guess I thought I'd graduate and get a job in Bronner. Something at the factory, maybe. I'd look pretty good building barbecues, right?" I pretend to screw something together, but Ashley frowns.

"Be serious. You're not even considering going to college?" I run my fingers through my hair.

"Nah, it's not for me. Not with these grades."

"You won't even try?"

"I'm going to stay here," I say quietly.

Ashley nods slowly; I think she can tell I don't want to talk about it. I throw up my hands. "Ah, look at us. Just a couple of messed-up teens in a nowhere town." I clink my plastic cup to hers. "Cheers," I say, and I toss back the rest of the melted ice cubes.

"I'll pay," Ashley tells me, pulling from her backpack an envelope that looks to be stuffed with bills.

I raise my eyebrows. "Wow. That's a lot more than I thought we'd taken." Ashley doesn't respond, but goes to the counter to pay the check. I don't bring it up again. What's done is done. *And who am I to judge?* I think.

Sliding back into the booth, she asks, "What now?" I check my watch; it's almost five o'clock, and people are starting to filter into Danny's for dinner.

"It's getting late. I should go home; my mom will be wondering where I am. You sleeping in the woods again?" Ashley nods.

We go to leave Danny's, but before we head out, I peel the lost license from the side of the bar. Once on the sidewalk, Ashley looks at me curiously. "What's that?"

"Uh, a license," I say, pretending to study the card. "The address is for right around the corner."

"That's convenient. Should we drop it off?" Ashley asks.

"Yeah, I guess so." I navigate us to the address, where the

lawn still looks sad and the car is still parked in the driveway; then I hand the license to Ashley. "You want to do the honors?" She takes it and pops it into the mailbox.

We walk the bike down Main, which is starting to show signs of life. "You know, I've been wondering. With, like, a dollar to your name, how were you planning on surviving in the woods for longer than just one night?" I ask.

Ashley spreads out her hands. "The Lord provides," she says, and it's clear she's not joking.

I'm a bit surprised. "I kind of got the impression you weren't religious."

Ashley looks at me seriously. "I never said that. Religion . . ." she trails off as she stares down the sidewalk, ". . . is different for everyone. I don't think that's how it's supposed to be, but I think that's how it is." When I nod, she peers at me and asks, "Are you religious?"

I think about it. "More than I used to be. You live enough life and you have to be, a little bit." Trying to smile, I add, "The only thing I do know is that, if there is a God, He's got a sense of humor. I respect you for believing, though," I add quickly. "It takes a lot of guts to believe in anything, no matter what it is."

Ashley hops onto the crossbar, and I pedal us back to the Big6. It's not dark yet, but the air is turning a heavy gold, and the bugs are beginning to sing. "I love summer," she comments offhandedly. "I sit on the back porch and write as the sun sets. It's nice."

"Do you write a lot?" I ask.

She nods. "I do. When I was younger, I started to carry a notebook everywhere. That way, when I thought of a line of poetry or a story, I could write it down before it faded."

"Do you still do that?" I ask curiously. "Carry a notebook around?"

"I go through one every few months. I keep all my old notebooks in a corner under my bed."

"And then what do you do with them?"

Ashley shrugs. "I don't know. I haven't decided yet."

Looking into the evening, I tell her, "We used to play baseball on Saturday nights like this. Summertime used to be my favorite."

"It only used to be your favorite?"

After a moment's hesitation, I manage, "I'm getting kind of tired of it now. Something about the days being too long . . . they all blend together. Everything is starting to feel the same."

We get back to the Big6 after six o'clock. Dropping my bike by the side of the building, I tell her, "I'll walk you home."

"What a gentleman." We head into the woods, where we find the tree with the six Slim Jim wrappers. Ashley slides off her backpack and sits in the dirt, legs folded neatly beneath her.

"Am I, uh, going to see you tomorrow?" I ask.

"If you want to," she says. "You know where I am."

I wish her a good night and turn to head back to my bike. *It was a good day*, I think. *Everything considered*. Even if I won't fully admit it to myself, I'm disappointed Ashley isn't the change I wanted her to be—that her presence today was still because of something I did. But I was stupid to hope for something else.

I pop back into the Big6 to give Peety his glasses, which are lying on the curb outside. He thanks me, as usual.

———————

I don't get home until late. I can tell Mom is glad I'm back, but she doesn't want to say anything.

"Have a busy day?" she asks as she shovels a gelatinous mound of casserole onto a plate, handing it over.

"I did."

She peers at my face. "You've got a heck of a sunburn coming in. Were you outside a lot?"

"Yeah. Most of the day."

We sit and eat in front of the TV for a while, but I can't finish my meal. Mom looks at me. "You always finish your dinner," she says, worried.

"I had a big lunch, and we ate late."

"'We?'"

I shift uncomfortably in my seat. Nothing gets by her. "Yeah. I went to Danny's with a friend."

"Shanna?" Mom asks, surprised.

"No . . . Mom, I'm going to bed." I stick the rest of my casserole in the fridge and say goodnight.

I brush my teeth and take a shower. Lying in bed, I close my eyes for a second, before opening them and walking back to the top of the stairs.

"Can I do a load of laundry?" I call down. Mom gets off the couch and stands at the foot of the stairs.

"Are you sure you're feeling all right?"

"I'll go get my clothes."

———————

There are people, people everywhere. I'm at a beach somewhere, a rocky strip of shore where bodies thrum and throb in the light given off by a bonfire. I have a cup in my hand, red and plastic. Or maybe it's a can, I'm not sure. It doesn't matter—nothing matters but the music and the people and the flickering of the firelight over the water and the faces of the crowd.

I'm talking to people. They're talking to me, and we're laughing. Someone hands me another cup. I'm having a great night. There's music. These people are my friends.

This is a dream, but it's also a kind of memory. Lots of nights mashed up into one like a mixtape, the hot nights, the bonfires, the highlights and the gist of it. The summers, the music, the friends.

Someone comes up behind me, taps me on the shoulder. "Sam," they say. I know this voice, I know this person, but I don't turn around.

The dream starts to slide sideways.

The people around me are no longer smiling. They're no longer laughing. They're looking at me, the whole beach is, looking at me like they see into me, see through me.

"Bad duck," they say to me. I take a step back, then another. "Bad duck," they say again. "Bad duck, bad duck, bad duck."

The mantra washes over me like a wave, and I panic. I try to run, but I run in that dream-state way, running, running, never going anywhere.

Finally, I make it to the water, jumping in.

SUNDAY

I wake with a start. I'm hot and my skin is clammy. I put my face in my hands as I sit up on my bed. I remember only bits and fragments of my dream, but I push them aside. *No use thinking about it.*

My clock says it's a little before nine o'clock, which is later than I wanted, but yesterday was a long, hot, tiring day. I should have seen this coming. *Should have set an alarm,* I think, mentally kicking myself as I hop out of bed. Clean clothes are piled in a hamper outside my room, so I pull out some shorts and try to find a T-shirt to wear. I pull out a shirt, but—*not that one,* I think, and pull out another. *This one?* Who cares? Why does it matter? They're all shirts.

Downstairs, Mom drinks coffee as I make toast and pack my backpack for the day ahead. She looks me up and down. "You going anywhere in particular?"

"Meeting a friend. Maybe go to the . . . T-ball game."

"Hmm. Same friend as yesterday?"

"Yeah. Same as yesterday."

Mom nods but doesn't say anything. I wonder what she's thinking.

Outside, the wind ruffles my hair as I pedal. I've been sick of summer for a while, sick of the days that never end and the heat that sticks to you like a fog. Even the gold in the air and the trees loses its luster eventually. But today feels different than the others. More alive, somehow. I think about our heist from the day before and realize that, for the first time in a long time, I'm excited about something.

It's embarrassing, so I push the thought away. Blocks pass in a slow slide until I eventually pull in front of the Big6. It's getting close to ten as I drop my bike in the grass and follow the path through the woods to Ashley's tree.

She's not there. Her Slim Jim wrappers still stand like sentinels in a row, tied to a branch. I call her name a couple times, but her things aren't there either. A nervous prickle starts up the back of my neck. I'm not sure what to do, so I head out of the woods and around the Big6, coming to the front door.

As I push the glass door open, I hear the tinkle of the bell announcing my arrival and see Ashley talking to Peety.

"Hey there, sleeping beauty. You sure kept this young lady waiting," Peety says.

Smiling sheepishly, I tell Ashley, "I went out back but didn't see you."

"Worried, were you?" Peety asks with a mischievous smile.

I ignore him and walk up to her. "Sorry I'm late. I slept in. I guess I was more tired than I thought."

"It's all right," Ashley says. "I was talking with Peety." Turning back to him, she says, "Thank you for letting me use your phone. I'm going to wash up." As she heads toward the bathroom, Peety gives her a friendly smile, but he drops the act as soon as her back is turned. As she rounds the corner, he whispers to me intently.

"I'm worried about that girl. She says she's sleeping in the woods back behind the shop. Did you know that?"

I nod. "Yeah, Peety. I know."

"Why? Hasn't she got a family?"

"She has a family."

Peety throws up his hands in exasperation. "Then tell me, why is she sleeping in the dirt at the back of my gas station?"

I exhale slowly, doing my best not to make it too conspicuous. "I don't know. I think it's complicated." Peety looks at me, unimpressed. "Peety, I don't know her very well. I think she's going back home soon, anyway. I know she has a plan—she told me she's not sleeping outside forever. Hey, who was she on the phone with, anyway?"

"Not sure. Sounded like it might have been a—"

Just then, Ashley rounds the corner from the bathroom. Peety pivots conversation topics, straightening up and putting his hands on his hips. "Another real scorcher today."

"When's it not?" I ask.

"Seems like summer gets longer every year," Peety says. I snort. *You don't know the half of it.*

Ashley waves at Peety as we head outside. He waves back, but I see him frowning through his facade. *Peety's always worrying*, I think, then turn my thoughts to the church.

"Hey, Ashley, there's something I need to do today. I was wondering if you wanted to come with me?"

This piques her curiosity. "What are you doing?"

"I actually have to go to a church. The Episcopalian one to the south of town. I hope that's not—"

"No," Ashley says quickly. "Our church is in Bronner."

"Okay, well, I have to be there by ten forty for an errand. Will you come with me?"

"It beats sitting on the ground by myself."

Relieved, I tell her, "Hop on, then. We'll get going."

"What exactly do you have to do at this church?" Ashley asks as I start to pedal.

I scramble to think of a reason. "I, uh, have to drop something off. My mom asked me to."

Ashley accepts this without question, and I bike hard, cutting southwest across town. A while later, we come to the church. I lean the bike to the side of the door and check my watch. It's just before ten forty. I'm hot and tired, but I made it in time. "Will you wait out here for a second? It won't take long."

Ashley nods. I go to push the door open when she calls out, "You don't need this?" She hands me my backpack, which I pretend to have forgotten.

"Oh, yeah. Thanks. I'll be back in a minute."

Inside the building, I creep to the platter of blond peanut butter brownies. I hear people upstairs, but I'm alone for now. I pick up the plate and go to put it in the garbage, but then I stop. There's a four-year-old with a severe peanut allergy—a Cole or a Caleb, some name like that—who's going to get his sticky little kid-fingers on these if I don't make the platter disappear. But Ashley and I don't have that problem, and it seems a shame to let them all go to waste, so I take two pieces from the platter before throwing the rest away.

I move to leave, but realize it's only been a few seconds. I'd said I'd be quick, but that's a suspiciously short amount of time to deliver something. I wait there for a minute longer before heading outside, handing one of the brownies to Ashley. "Where did you get this?" she asks.

I shrug. "Someone gave them to me. So, what do we want to do today? We've got options. We could . . ." I peter out, realizing our choices are actually extremely limited. "Hmm. There are *some* options. There's T-ball at the school, because I know how much you love hot dogs. There's the hardware store, where we have the world's most expensive necklace—"

"How much is the necklace?" Ashley asks, interrupting.

"Six hundred and fifty dollars."

"I doubt that's the world's most expensive necklace."

"You're probably right. Well, maybe it's the most expensive necklace sold in a hardware store. Okay, we don't have to see the necklace. There's the library, the lake again, Danny's, the Searchlight . . . we could sit around the Big6 and eat Slim Jims all day. Anything sound good?"

"I'd like to go to Name Rock," Ashley says, catching me off guard.

I try not to let my surprise leak into my voice. "Name Rock? Why there?"

She shrugs. "I hear people talking about it. It sounds interesting."

"I don't know if 'interesting' is how I'd describe it. More like a trashed-up monument to high school stupidity," I tell her, doing my best to play it off.

"Ah," she says. "So you've been."

"It's been a while. It's . . . by Stevens Point Lake."

"That's what I've heard." She gets flustered all of a sudden. "Unless you'd rather not go. I didn't mean—"

"It's fine," I tell her. "If you want to go to Name Rock, we'll go to Name Rock." Smiling thinly, I motion for her to get on my bike.

"You know," I say as we take off, "that necklace, the one that was six hundred and fifty dollars, was also a rock."

"Don't most necklaces have rocks?"

"Yeah, but this one was a rock-rock. Like, a rock you find in the dirt."

"Really?" Ashley asks, curious.

"Yep. Mr. Coen—that's the owner of the hardware store— says that his brother was fixing fences at his uncle's farm when, out of nowhere, this rock hit him on the head. Mr. Coen says the area around his brother was flat, there was nowhere the rock could have fallen from. So, his brother picks up the rock and puts it in his pocket. That evening, the brother meets the lady who eventually becomes his wife. Mr. Coen says his brother always thought the rock was lucky."

"If it's so lucky, why is it being sold?"

Smiling, I reply, "You know, I've got the same question," and pedal along.

"Do you believe in luck?" Ashley asks me.

"What do you mean?"

"Do you think there are people things always go right for? Do you think some people have it easier?"

"Like the universe is giving them a break? Hmm. I have a cousin who never loses at cards. Doesn't matter what it is—hearts, poker, even Uno, he never loses. I guess I do believe in luck. Well, *good* luck, I guess I believe in. *Bad* luck, I believe in for sure."

"Why's that?"

I think on that one. "I think some people get the butt end of the universe. No matter what they do, no matter who they are or how they try to wiggle out of it, some people are just plain cursed. I think bad luck," I continue, "really the heart of it, is the fact that, even if you don't deserve it, the universe doesn't care." I pause and shake my head. "The universe doesn't care about you, or what hobbies you have, or if you're a good person or not, or how much money you make. It'll crush you anyway." Shrugging, I finish, "And some people get the short stick more than others."

"So, Sam Riley. Do you have bad luck?" I wish I could see Ashley's face. I want to know what she's thinking.

"Maybe. Some days it sure feels like it. Bad luck for a bad duck." I smile humorlessly. "Why? Do you believe in luck?"

"I'm religious. That means I can't."

I smile for real this time. "You know, I always forget that. With the stealing of the money, and all." I'm joking—the conversation has rattled me—but Ashley doesn't say anything, and I think I've hurt her feelings. "I'm sorry. I don't mean it.

I just mean that . . . I don't understand why we did that. And it's none of my business, anyway. It doesn't make you . . ." I fumble for the words. ". . . a bad person, or anything."

"People are complicated," Ashley says quietly.

"Yeah. I'm beginning to see that." We coast in silence for a while.

"You know," I say after a few minutes, "I went to Stevens Point a few summers ago." I pause for a second to collect my story. "It was the first time I'd been. The seniors were throwing a bonfire, but I didn't drink yet. I still thought drinking was for the 'bad kids,' but one of my older cousins had given me some good advice. He told me that if you're not drinking, you should find a cup and carry it around. That way, no one will pressure you to get a beer, and you don't have to tell people you're not drinking every time someone asks if you want one." Looking at the top of Ashley's head, I can't tell what she's thinking, so I continue the story. "So I found a mostly empty cup and carried it around with me almost the whole night. At the end of the night, I started talking to this girl and she asked me why my cup was almost empty, so to look really cool, I tossed the rest back. But it wasn't beer—turns out it was spit from the dip someone had been chewing. I almost puked. She didn't want to talk to me after that."

"Wow. That's revolting."

"I think I was sick for two straight days afterward. It was probably . . . what's the word? Where you think something is actually happening to you, but it's all in your brain?"

"Psychosomatic."

"Yeah, that's the one. It was a long time before I tried to drink again. And when I finally did, I made sure I opened the can myself."

"Is that the kind of person you are? A party animal?"

Shrugging, I tell her, "I used to be. My dad might be a cop, but I've lived here my whole life. I had a lot of friends. I made the circuits."

"'Had' a lot of friends? 'Made' the circuits? That's past tense."

"Yeah. I, uh, don't get out as much as I used to. I've got a lot on my mind."

"A lot on your mind? You told me you're failing math. If you're thinking, it's not about school."

"Ah, you got me there." I shake my finger at Ashley. "Anyone ever tell you you're a smart cookie?"

"Not in so many words."

After another moment's silence, I tell her, "All right. I've been doing a lot of talking. I told you my most embarrassing story. Now you have to tell me more about yourself."

"That was your most embarrassing story? I may not know you very well, but I don't believe that."

"Fine. Not my *most* embarrassing, but it's up there. Hey, though, stop changing the subject."

I used to be good at talking to people. I used to be charismatic and popular, a guy people would want to tell things to. And today, here in nowhere America, this midmorning with the birds chirping and the sky shining, I feel like I might be that person again.

"It has to be an embarrassing story?" she asks.

"Sure. If you want."

She chews her lip for a second. "A couple years ago, I set a tablecloth on fire in the middle of service."

"Wow," I say. "That's . . . yeah. Pretty embarrassing."

"It was an accident. I tipped over one of our Lent candles. First the dried flowers caught fire, then the tablecloth. Someone pulled it off the table and stamped it out. There's still a burn mark on the carpet. I do feel bad when I look at it."

"Jeez. Talk about a rough morning."

"Yeah. I was grounded for a weekend for being 'reckless and inattentive.' But Melissa snuck me a bunch of candy from the front desk of the office my dad works in, so it wasn't all bad."

We talk for a long time, after that. She tells me about her past. She tells me about her future too, who she wants to be someday. She says she wants to write poetry and live in a house with a wraparound porch and a rocking chair, one she'll sit in every night to drink tea and eat Slim Jims.

"Slim Jims? Really?"

"Sometimes. Most nights I'll have a charcuterie."

"I don't think that's a real word."

"Please, Sam, get a dictionary."

She says her house will have a conservative four bedrooms; one will be used as a study, one will be a master bedroom, and the other two will be filled with plants.

"No beds in the other bedrooms?"

"Of course, there will be beds. Otherwise, I would have said one bedroom."

"There's even going to be a bed in the study?"

"Yes. The study will have a daybed."

"See, I don't think that's a word, either."

Ignoring this, she continues, "There will be beds for guests. Like Lissa, when she comes to visit."

Hearing that name, I grow curious. "Okay, so you want to be a poet. What does your sister want to do?"

"She's an actress. She's beautiful and talented," Ashley says, tucking a stray piece of hair behind her ear. She says this directly, like she's stating a fact.

"That's amazing. I don't think I've ever met an actress. What does she act in?"

"I don't know. She lives in New York City; I've not seen her in a long time. We don't get to talk often."

"Oh. I'm sorry. I hope you can see her soon."

"I hope so too."

We're almost at the edge of the woods. I tell Ashley we have to walk the rest of the way and she looks at her feet, dejectedly. She's wearing a worn pair of old Converse.

"You didn't bring your hiking boots?" I ask.

"I didn't know I'd be needing them."

As she heads toward the woods, I stare at her ponytail, which swishes back and forth as she walks.

She turns to look at me. "Are you sure you're okay with this?" she asks.

I fidget uncomfortably. "Yeah. Sure. Why wouldn't I be?" I tell her. "Let's get going."

Ashley looks at me for a long second with her dark cat eyes before making her way into the woods.

———

We walk for a long way. The path is pretty well worn. We're lucky it hasn't rained recently—it can get wet and marshy after a hard rainfall. I tell Ashley that one time I was walking this way when the path was muddy, only to lose my footing on the side of a hill and slide fifteen feet through the underbrush.

She smiles. "When I was little," she says, staring up the path, "we had a dog named Georgie. He was a cocker spaniel. When it rained and I came inside, he would lick the mud off my shoes. My mother had to start keeping our rainboots in the pantry."

"I've never had a dog," I tell her. "Dad says they're too much work."

"All the good things are. How much farther to Name Rock?" she asks, changing the subject.

"Three-quarters of a mile. Maybe a little more. Your feet hurt?" She nods. "It had to be far enough out where the adults wouldn't catch us. I mean, they know we're out here, but what are they going to do? Hike a mile at night to catch us drinking in the woods? Nah, they've all got other things to worry about. Like their arthritis. They wouldn't make it."

"This seems like it would be treacherous when it's dark. How did you leave at the end of the night?"

"A lot of times, I didn't."

"What do you mean?" she asks curiously.

"Uh," I say, combing my fingers through my hair, "there's a shack out here. I'd sleep there sometimes."

"Seems I'm not the only one who's spent some time sleeping in the woods."

"I had a cot, though. A little more comfortable than the cold, hard ground."

"I can assure you, it is the opposite of cold," she says, and I smile.

"I believe you," I tell her. "Well, a lot of the guys had ATVs and could get back pretty easily. There are tons of trails out here."

"Don't the trails all look the same at night?"

"No. A few of us took it upon ourselves to conduct a community service project a year or so ago. We got some solar-powered lights and set them up along a couple of the more popular paths to keep the newbies from getting lost. Plus, everyone brings a flashlight."

"That's resourceful. Think about what you could accomplish if you spent that much effort on your schoolwork."

"Pssh. Okay, Mom."

"Do you have more stories?" Ashley asks. "I'd like to hear some." Her voice drops. "If you'd like, I've heard telling stories about someone is a way to—"

Clearing my throat loudly, I say quickly, "Yeah, I've got a ton of great stories. One time, Bryce lost a bet. He got the lowest score bowling at the alley in Bronner, so he had to toss his whole wallet in the lake, driver's license and all."

Her eyes widen. "Bryce Whise? From our class? He did not live up to his last name."

"The one and only. But it's not all bad. Three days later, it showed up on the bench outside of school. Nothing was missing from it. It just appeared."

"That's incredible," Ashley marvels.

"Yeah, Bryce is a really lucky guy. He told me once that as a kid—five years old, maybe—he got lost on a hike with his family around Gooseberry Lake. He walked and walked until he was exhausted and fell asleep. When he woke up, he was by his family's car at the trailhead."

"Wow," Ashley says. "Do you believe that?"

I laugh. "I didn't used to. But these days—who knows?"

If that was a weird thing to say, Ashley doesn't comment. I notice she seems to be thinking. "I didn't know these things about our classmates, the stories you're telling me. Isn't it strange? How you can spend so much time with people and still not know them at all?"

"Ashley, I have to say, they're great people. You just have to get to know them." I pause for a second. "I know they'd love you if you gave them a chance. I mean, we've been in the same class for years, and I hadn't really gotten to know you before this weekend. And now look at us. On a grand adventure to Name Rock."

She looks at me inscrutably, then turns back to stare up the path. "Hmm. You may be right. Frankly, I'm surprised at the person you turned out to be."

"Oh, yeah? And what does that mean?"

"I'd thought you didn't care about anything. Now, I think you care about everything. And everyone," she adds, then changes the subject. "Are we close?"

"Yep. We're just about there. It's at the bottom of this hill."

We've been walking for quite a while. Stevens Point Lake is north of Redford a mile or so. It has one big public beach that's the go-to spot for families during the summer and a few houses scattered here and there on the shoreline, but mostly it's wooded hills and stretches of short, rocky beaches. A lot of the land surrounding the lake is private but almost none is developed.

Descending the hill, we break through the tree line into a plateaued area, which has been intentionally cleared of trees and brush. In the middle is a large firepit, around which several beaten and weather-worn plastic chairs stand watch. To our left there's a steep slope; at its bottom is a short run of rocky beach that tapers into gently lapping water. A small handful of cans are scattered about the site haphazardly. Fragments of last night's dream surface, but I push them away.

"Come on, guys. Pick up your trash," I mutter, distracting myself. I gather the cans and toss them into the firepit as Ashley wanders about the makeshift party site.

"It's . . . cleaner than I thought it would be," she says.

I shrug. "We do our best."

"What's that?" She points to something bobbing in the wind, at the end of a long branch that hangs over the lake.

"It's a rope swing."

"I've never used one," she says.

I stare at Ashley, dumbfounded. "You've lived here your whole life, and you've never used a rope swing?"

"Never."

"Okay. Well, there's no time like the present, right?"

"Sam," she says seriously. "It's a death trap. I am not getting on that."

"Of course you are! You have to. What are you, afraid of fun?" She shakes her head. "Come on, Ashley. It's not summer without a rope swing."

Looking at it seriously, she asks, "Has anyone ever died on it?"

The question startles me. "What? No—no, of course not," I say quickly.

"Has anyone been injured?"

"I mean, nothing more than a few bruises," I tell her—it's the truth.

She bites her lip but nods her head slowly. "Fine. One time only."

"Great! I'll get it for you. You're not going to regret this," I yell to her as I climb the tree, a giant thing with limbs splitting off in every direction. "I'm going to swing the rope to you, and you have to grab it. Okay?"

I swing the rope and Ashley reaches out, catching it as it passes by. I've done that same thing many, many times.

I'm holding the rope and looking out at the lake.

"You have to let go at the end of the swing, or you won't get as far," a voice tells me.

"I know that. Besides, I shouldn't be taking advice from you. I saw you fall off and land on the bank last weekend," I hear myself say.

The voice laughs. "Don't remind me. I still hurt."

I climb down from the tree.

"Are you okay?" Ashley asks. "You look a bit pale."

I manage a smile. "I don't know how that could be possible, under this sunburn."

"Sam, we don't have to be here. We can go back to the Big6 and get some lunch."

Fidgeting awkwardly, I tell her, "It's okay. We're here already."

"I shouldn't have asked you to come," she says, but I don't want to talk about it.

"It's fine. Really."

I can tell Ashley doesn't believe me, but she sits on the beach and unties her shoes anyway, placing them next to her backpack. Standing, she announces, "I'm ready."

"Okay. So, what you're going to do is take this rope and stand as far back from the edge as possible. Then, you run toward the beach and use your upper-body strength to lift yourself up with the rope as best as you can, swinging over the water. When you can't hold on any longer, you let go. Got it?"

Nodding, she takes the rope, stepping a couple lengths back and then running toward the lake with a cry. She doesn't make it very far, splashing gracelessly into the water with a yelp. When her head bobs up, I'm laughing.

"That was great," I yell to her. "Want to do it again?"

Shaking her head, she paddles her way back. Pulling herself up onto the beach, she lays her head in the rocky sand and looks up at me. "Once is enough." She pulls herself to an elbow and eyes the lake. "I didn't make it very far."

"It doesn't matter. You made a big splash, that's what counts."

Ashley lies back against the beach. "When do I get to see the rock?" she asks.

"Uh, well. You can see the rock whenever you want. It's off in the woods a little way. Are you going to put your name on it?" I climb down the steep slope and sit next to her.

"Why would I do that?"

"Where do you think 'Name Rock' comes from? When seniors graduate, they put their name on the rock. Some of the names are pretty old."

"What do they use to write with?"

"Most people use a Sharpie. It doesn't last as long, but it's the thought that counts."

"I thought it was the splash that counts?" she says.

I smile. "It depends on what we're talking about."

"Exactly what is the thought, anyway?"

"That you're done. That this part of your life is finished. It's bittersweet, I guess," I say with a shrug.

Ashley stands up. "Let's go, then."

A few dozen feet into the woods, there's a sort of rocky cliffside that extends upward from us. Names are written on the rock face, some etched with penknives, some painted or left in permanent marker. A few are fresh but most are faded. There are lots of names overlapping at the bottom of the rock face, but their numbers thin out as you look farther up.

Ashley walks to the wall and traces names with her fingers.

"I know some of these people. Sean lives a few houses down. Marcie sits next to me in geometry."

Marcie, I think.

I'm standing on a sidewalk. Marcie and I are having a conversation. Someone else is there too. "How's coaching T-ball?" I ask.

She shrugs. "It's okay. Kids are hard. It's like hurting cats."

"Wait, what did you say?" I ask, confused.

"It's like hurting cats," she repeats.

The third voice laughs. "It's 'herding cats,' Marcie. Not hurting them."

"Yeah," I say with a laugh. "What did the cats ever do to you?"

Ashley must have noticed my mind is elsewhere. "You okay, Sam?"

I shake it off. "Yeah. So, what do you think? You want to add your name?"

Ashley considers this. "Where's your name?" she asks.

Doing my best not to betray nerves, I search the rock face for my addition. "Here," I tell her, pointing to a small "Sam Riley" that's been etched crudely near where a small point juts from the face. *Bad duck,* I think, as I pass my fingers over the rough letters of my name.

Ashley looks at it. "Your penmanship could use some work."

I smile but it's without humor. "You're not the first person who's told me that. So, are you going to add your name, or did we come all the way out here for nothing?" Either way, I'm eager to get going.

"I think . . . I think I will." She pulls a thick permanent marker from her backpack.

"You come prepared. Okay, then. Once you put your name on the rock, it means you're done with whatever your life looks like today, and you're ready for tomorrow. It's a big moment. You ready for it?"

Ashley looks at me, considering. "When I put my name on this, it means I'm leaving the past behind?"

"I mean, not to be overly dramatic, but sure. I guess you could say that." She nods, removes the cap of the marker, and closes her eyes, looking very much like she's making a wish before she blows out candles on a birthday cake. Then she turns to the rock and writes her name in small cursive letters on the face near the bottom.

Replacing the cap, she turns back to me. "That felt nice," she says.

"It looked like you were making a wish," I tell her as we head back to the clearing with the plastic chairs and the bon-fire pit.

"It felt a little like that," she says with a small smile.

"Are you going to tell me what you wished for?"

"No. I'm not."

I shrug. "That's fair. If you tell me, it might not happen."

At this, Ashley simply nods. Then, suddenly, she says, "I'd like to try the rope swing again."

"Yeah?" I arch my eyebrow. "All right. I'll go get it for you, then."

I climb the tree as she strips off her shoes, then swing her the rope, which she catches deftly. She walks several long paces backward from the waterline, looks out at the lake with the concentration of a sprinter on a starting block, and with a great yell runs toward the lake, picking herself up off the ground before swinging over the water. At the height of the pendulum, she drops into the water with a magnificent splash.

She paddles back to shore, where I give her a round of applause. She's smiling brightly, and her hair is plastered to her forehead. "How did I do?"

"You win 'most improved.' That was impressive." Putting her shoes back on, she tells me she's ready to leave for real this time.

"I don't think I've ever seen you smile like that," I tell her as we start to make our way out of the woods.

"What do you mean?"

"When you came out of the water. You looked happy."

Ashley looks at me. "I am happy," she says.

"I'm . . . really glad to hear that."

"And you, Sam? Are you happy?"

"Right now? Yeah," I tell her, and I realize it's true.

"Nothing lasts, though, does it?" Ashley says absently.

"No. It doesn't."

"*C'est la vie.*"

"What is that? French?" I ask.

"Yes. It means 'such is life.' My grandmother used to say it to me."

"Your grandmother sounds like a nice person."

"She wasn't," Ashley says, but doesn't elaborate.

We walk in silence for a while. I look at my watch; it's getting close to three. I tell Ashley I'm tired, and she agrees it has been a long weekend. It strikes me that if I'm tired, she must be exhausted. I've at least gotten decent sleep; she's been sleeping on the ground for two straight nights in the summer heat. When I tell her this, though, she simply shrugs. "Nothing to be done."

We're walking and talking, almost out of the woods. Ashley is behind me when I hear a yelp. I turn around to see her on the ground, clutching a gash on her shin.

"Are you okay?" I ask as I jog back to her, concerned. Leaning down, I look at her leg.

"I tripped. It's bleeding, but it's not deep." I have no medical experience, but I think she's right. She pulls the backpack off her back and rummages around in it, blood dripping slowly from the gash on her leg.

Drip. Drip. Drip. I stare at it, hypnotized, as it pools in the dry dirt of the forest floor before being slowly absorbed into the dark, growing stain of mud. I think about Mrs. Van Slyke. I think about the wine soaking into the tablecloth. I think about—I don't think about anything else. I push all the thoughts away. Still, I start to feel queasy again.

"Sam," Ashley says, breaking me from my trance. "Do you have any water?" I pull out what's left of the bottle, and she goes to pour it over the gash, but stops. "I can't get the angle right. Will you do it?"

She hands the bottle to me. I look at it, then at the gash. I swallow hard.

Ashley must see something is wrong. "Are you all right?"

"I'm not . . . not feeling great," I stammer.

"It's okay." Ashley takes the bottle back from me, contorts herself awkwardly over her shin and pours the water over her leg. Then she wraps and ties a T-shirt from her backpack over the gash. "That will work for a while." She puts her hand on my shoulder and uses me to stand up, warbling a bit as she tests her leg.

"How is it?"

"Passable. How far is your bike?"

"It's right over there." I motion in front of us. "Can you make it that far?"

"Unless you carry me, I don't have a choice."

Looking down at my hands, I begin, "Sure, I can—"

"It was a joke, Sam. I'll be okay." She hobbles up the path and I follow, eventually breaking through the trees and to the bike.

"How's the T-shirt holding up?" I ask.

"Not well. I need a bandage."

"We're pretty far out of town, but we could go to the hardware store. I bet they'd have bandages." Ashley sits on the ground by the bike and I look at her—really look at her. I can tell she's exhausted. She hasn't slept in two days, and she's probably eaten nothing but junk food. At the very least, she needs real food and a place to rest for a while.

"Why don't we go to my house?" I ask.

Ashley looks up at me, surprised. "Your house?"

"Yeah. My mom will be home soon, she'll know how to fix you up. Plus, we're having tacos for dinner."

Ashley chews on her lip nervously. "I don't know—"

"Come on. You're exhausted. You need to eat, and we need someone to look at your leg." When she still looks nervous, I add, "My mom isn't going to tell your parents, I promise."

"It's not your mom I'm worried about."

After a moment, I realize what she's saying. "My dad isn't home, either. He's . . . not coming home tonight."

Finally, Ashley slowly nods. "Okay."

"All right, then. It's settled." I start to pick my bike off the ground, but I see the T-shirt on Ashley's leg is already starting to side off. I sit next to her and motion toward her leg. "Mind if I take a look?"

She moves her leg toward me, and I pull off the T-shirt, doing my best to not look at the cut itself. I rewrap the shirt as tightly as possible, then pull the shoestring out of my sneaker and wrap that up and down over the bandage on her leg, tying it in a bow. "Your shoe will fall off," she tells me.

"Maybe," I say. "But that T-shirt won't." I walk the bike up to the road and motion for her to hop on, which she does with a little difficulty. "It'll probably take us a little more than half an hour to get home. Think you can hold on for that long?"

Ashley nods, and we take off.

———

I pedal faster than I should, but it's okay—I've gotten used to having another person on the bike, and I want to get Ashley to the house as soon as possible. It's been a long day for both of us. I'm not looking forward to seeing Mom, but it doesn't matter. Bringing Ashley home is the right decision.

I realize I have another problem, though. Ryan, the lost boy. I'm almost late for him. *Crap*, I think. *Crap, crap, crap.*

If I get lucky, we might run into him on the way. I check my watch—it's about three thirty. I've done this enough times, I think I know where he'll be.

We take a bit of an odd way home, swinging more west than we need to, and sure enough—we come upon a street corner where a little boy is crying, sitting on the edge of the curb, his face in his hands.

"Should we help him?" Ashley asks the question before I can.

"Will you be okay if we stop?"

She nods. "Of course. We can't leave him here," she says, and I realize she's right. I approach Ryan.

"Hey, Ryan. Hey, buddy. You lost?" I ask. He looks up—I can tell he doesn't recognize me. "Let's get you home," I tell him. I turn to Ashley. "I know where he lives. It won't take more than five minutes."

"I'll still be here," she says, setting herself gingerly on the curb.

I take Ryan's hand and lead him a few blocks away, bringing him to the door of his house and letting him inside before ducking out quickly. When I jog back, Ashley is still waiting on the street corner. I hop back on my bike and motion for her to do the same.

"Do you know that boy?" she asks, curious.

I shrug off the question. "He gets lost sometimes," I say, and I leave it at that.

A bit later, we peel up my driveway, and I stop the bike. Ashley dismounts from the crossbar and looks up at my house, crossing her arms. "Cute," she says.

I walk up the steps to the front door. Pushing it open, I head inside. "Mom?" I yell out.

"Hi, Sam. And—a friend?" She stops short when she sees Ashley walk through the doorway.

"Hello," Ashley says, somewhat awkwardly. "I'm Ashley Albert."

Mom comes over. "Albert? You live on Morrison Street?" She darts a look at me as Ashley nods. "It's nice to meet you. I'm Mrs. Riley. And you know Sam from . . ." She trails off, looking at me.

"School," I finish, before cutting to the chase. "Ashley got hurt—can you take a look at it?"

"Hurt?" Mom asks, concerned. She motions for Ashley to sit on one of the dining table chairs, then leans down and unties the shoestring, handing it to me. "I assume this is yours."

Carefully unpeeling the makeshift T-shirt bandage, she looks at the cut. I'm instructed to fetch some things from the bathroom vanity and bring them to her. When I return, Mom takes the hydrogen peroxide and cotton swabs I've gathered and uses them to clean the gash.

"It's not too deep, but it's long," she says as she dabs at the cut with a medicated cotton swab. "How'd you get this?"

"I fell as we were coming back from the lake."

"Gooseberry Lake?" Mom asks nonchalantly.

"Stevens Point," Ashley says, responding before I can.

Mom looks up at me, startled, but she recovers quickly and clears her throat. "And what were you doing all the way out there?"

"Nothing," I say quickly. "We were just hiking." Mom doesn't mention it again, but I can tell she's concerned. I'm used to looking at her and knowing how she's feeling, despite what she might say or how she acts. I've been her son for a long time. I can see it in the clouds in her eyes and the creases on her forehead. Still, she simply nods and continues to dab at the gash.

When she goes to wrap it with the bandage, she stops. "Would you like to take a shower?" she asks Ashley. "I feel bad cleaning only a part of you when it looks like all of you could use a wash."

Ashley looks at me, then nods, and Mom fetches her a towel and takes her to the bathroom. When the water starts running, Mom comes back. She looks at me, arms crossed in worry. "What is going on with that girl?" she asks.

I fidget uncomfortably. "What do you mean?"

"Sam. I can understand getting dirty in the woods, but she looks like she hasn't showered in days. She's as skinny as a reed. I've never heard you say her name before in your life, and then suddenly you bring her home. What is going on here?"

I wasn't prepared for questions like this. Shrugging awkwardly, I reply, "I know her from school. I saw her today and we hung out for a while."

"And you went to Stevens Point?"

"For a little bit."

Mom looks at me, her brow furrowing. "Sam, are you using drugs?"

I'm shocked. "Mom—what? No! Why would you even ask that?"

"You've been hanging out with . . . strange girls. She comes here hurt, you both come back *filthy*, and you've been"—she motions around her—"God knows where. What am I supposed to think?"

"I don't know, Mom, but not that."

"You've been acting strangely lately. Some of it I understand, but—I feel like you've become a different person."

I want to storm off, but I don't know where I'd go. "Mom, I don't want to talk about this. I'm *fine*. And I'm not 'using drugs,'" I tell her, making little air quotes with my fingers.

Mom looks like she wants to say something else, but she doesn't. Her shoulders slump a little. "Fine. I'm sorry. I believe you."

"Great. I'm going to take a shower too," I say through gritted teeth as I head upstairs.

I'm so angry. I've had a long day, a long weekend—a long *life*, lately—and I don't deserve this. *Ashley doesn't deserve it either.*

My shower is short and cold. Through the thin walls of the house, I can hear Ashley and Mom talking downstairs as I turn the water off. I pull on some clean clothes and catch a quick look at myself in the mirror. I'm so sunburned—I would hurt tomorrow, if there ever were one. Instead, it'll be just another Friday.

"Well, it was nice to meet you," Mom says as she sees me coming down the stairs. Ashley catches my eye, and I clear my throat.

"Actually, Mom, I thought Ashley might stay for dinner."

Frowning hard, Mom chooses her next words carefully.

"Sam, you know how your father feels about dinner guests," she says, an edge of caution in her voice.

"I know," I say, fidgeting. "But we've been out all day, and I bet Ashley is hungry. I know I am. Just this one time. Please?" I ask.

"I really don't think that's a good idea. Your father will be home soon."

"We'll eat quickly, I promise. Besides, when was the last time we had someone over for dinner?"

Mom looks uncomfortable, but a few long seconds later, she relents. "Fine. Will you set the table, then?" she asks, and throws a furtive glance at the clock.

———————

I set the table and we all sit for dinner, Mom saying grace. I peek at Ashley, who has her hands folded piously and her eyes screwed closed, a frown on her face.

We pass the food around and Mom makes small talk as I put a taco together. "How's your family?" she asks Ashley.

"They're well. My mom still helps at the church, and my dad is still working."

"And her sister lives in New York City," I finish for her.

Mom glances at me inscrutably, but Ashley doesn't react. "Does she? That's lovely." There's quiet for a second before she asks another inane question.

Dinner goes on like this until eventually the plates are cleared, Mom still making small talk. "What does your family do for fun?"

"We play a lot of Scrabble," Ashley says.

"Really? I used to play a lot of Scrabble when I was younger too," Mom tells us.

I have an idea, though maybe not a good one. "You guys want to play a round?" I ask.

Mom looks at me, confused. "You hate Scrabble."

Shrugging awkwardly, I say, "I thought it might be fun."

Frowning, Mom reminds me, "Your father will be home soon."

"He's always telling me I need to study more. Doesn't this count?" I ask.

Mom sighs. "I do love Scrabble," she says. "But only one round."

About halfway into the game, Ashley plays an S, an A, and a V on my ANT to create SAVANT. "Ah, a savant," Mom says. "What you're turning out to be in Scrabble."

"I wouldn't say that. I drew good tiles, that's all."

"So, you're lucky then?" Mom asks.

"I would not say that either," Ashley says as she watches my Mom play a six-tile word over a double-points space.

Mom smiles. "I also drew good tiles. This is a treat—Sam never plays Scrabble with me."

"And Mr. Riley?" Ashley asks.

Frowning, Mom looks at the clock on the wall. "Not much for words."

"Interesting. Sam told me English is his favorite subject; he must have gotten that from you. He told me it's the only subject he's not failing."

"Samuel!" Mom exclaims, concerned.

I put my hands up defensively. "It's a joke! It was a joke! I wasn't serious." I was serious. I am flunking my senior year—*Not that it matters,* I think. But I am not in the mood to have that conversation.

We wrap up the round with my mom pulling a slim lead over Ashley, while I come in at an unsurprising third place. I can tell Mom is having fun, and I'm glad to see it. Still, I catch her once again looking at the clock in the living room.

Ashley stands up suddenly. "Would you mind if I use your phone?"

Mom points her to the phone on the wall by the kitchen and tells her it's no problem at all. Ashley walks to it and dials a number with slow precision; picking the phone off the cradle, she walks it into the kitchen and out of sight, stretching the cord as far as it will go.

Mom looks at me curiously, as if to ask who she's calling. "You'll be heading out now?" she asks instead.

"I thought we could play another round."

"I don't think so, Sam. That's not a good idea."

"We could break out that ice cream we didn't get around to eating on my birthday." Mom looks at me warily. "Dad loves ice cream," I say. "He can have some when he gets back."

Mom frowns again, but then smiles. "I am having a lot of fun."

"I know."

She gets the ice cream—vanilla, my favorite. I set the bowls and spoons on the table, and Mom doles out dessert as Ashley walks from the kitchen and hangs up the phone.

"Calling your parents?" says my mom. "That's a good idea, it's getting to be late." When Ashley doesn't respond to the question, she adds, "How do you feel about one more round over dessert?"

"That would be great," Ashley says. "Are you playing?" she asks me.

"Of course he is. The worst he can get is third place, right?" Mom says.

Smiling, Ashley replies, "I also see where Sam gets his sense of humor."

Mom looks at me curiously. "I'm glad he's making jokes to someone. The most I can get out of him is a grunt sometimes."

It's another knockdown, drag-out fight between Ashley and my mom—I once again come in third, but not by as wide of a margin as I had the first time. By the end of the night, Mom is laughing and Ashley is smiling, and I'm smiling too. It's a lighter mood than we've had in the house for a long time.

But all good things must come to an end. Mom looks at the clock and frowns again. It's past eight thirty. "Sam, it's getting late. You'd better walk Ashley home." She turns to Ashley. "Thank you for coming over tonight. It was wonderful having you. We don't often have guests, so this has been—" she catches my eye, and finishes, "—nice."

"Thank you for having me. It was . . . really wonderful," Ashley says, and I can tell she's being sincere.

"Take care of your leg," Mom tells her a few minutes later, as she waves us off. I pick up my bike, and we start to walk down the road.

———————

"That was lovely," Ashley says as soon as we're out of earshot. "Thank you for inviting me. It's been a long time since I've had such fun."

Grinning, I reply, "You just liked using me as a Scrabble punching bag."

Ashley smiles, and we walk together in silence. It's going to be dark soon, and the night bugs are starting to chatter.

"I love the nighttime," she tells me after a while. "It's peaceful." I think about the nights I've spent on my bike and with my friends, laughing over each other. I don't remember the specifics, but I remember the feeling. Free, in a way. "I appreciate the stars," she continues. "They make me feel insignificant. It puts things in perspective."

"Yeah? What kind of things?" I ask.

She shrugs. "Everything."

"I can understand that. It's like—in the face of eternity, what does it matter what you had for lunch, or who you went to prom with? It's kind of comforting."

"Well put, Sam Riley," she says, and I motion for her to hop up on the bike.

"I'm taking you back to the Big6?" I ask.

"You are."

"How much longer do you think you'll be out there?"

"Not for long."

"You, uh, going to tell me what your plan is?"

"I will," she says, "but not now," and I guess that'll have to do.

The sun's down, but the humidity is still a wet, oppressive blanket. I'm sweating already, and I hope Ashley doesn't notice. I ask her if she minds the heat. "I'm sure I don't mind it as much as you do; I'm not the one pedaling." A beat passes in the conversation before she continues. "I realized I've not thanked you for biking me everywhere, which must have been exhausting."

Again, she pauses. "I suppose what I'm really thanking you for is for spending the last two days with me. So, thank you for everything, Sam."

My face is getting hot again. "No problem. To be honest, it's been a long time since I've had so much fun. Things have been . . . rough, these last couple days."

"Days?" Ashley asks. I realize she wouldn't understand, so I just shrug. "I'm sorry to hear that," she says. After thinking for a second, she continues. "I think life is strange in that way. There are these stretches where everything is miserable, and you can't imagine what a light at the end of the tunnel would even begin to look like. And then it passes, and soon those bad days seem like a dream, like they never happened. But when you're in the middle of it, those days last forever. I think, Sam, that you are in one of those stretches."

As I pedal, I take a deep breath, hold it for a second, and let it out. She's right. *More than she knows,* I think.

"Thank you," I tell her. "That means a lot. Is it the same for you right now?"

Ashley sighs. "It is," she says. "But the important thing to remember is that it will get better."

"You're pretty optimistic for a girl who lives in the woods."

"It's not optimism. It's faith."

I smile ruefully. "Yeah. Maybe," I tell her. "Look at us. Two bad ducks."

"Yes," she says. "Two bad ducks."

We've arrived at the Big6. Pulling up to the picnic table, I hop off, Ashley doing the same, and lean the bike against the side of the table. Sweat has plastered my hair to my forehead. I wipe my hand across my brow, which comes away slick and wet. "I could really use some more of that ice cream right now," I say.

"The ice cream was great. I can't remember the last time I had ice cream."

"No ice cream for you when you were grounded on your birthday last year?"

"No ice cream for me," Ashley echoes. For a second, she chews on her lip. "I didn't do it, you know."

"Didn't do what?" I ask, confused.

"What I was grounded for. Cutting the ribbons from the page markers."

"And you didn't say that to anyone? You didn't tell them it wasn't you?"

"Some fights aren't worth fighting," she says.

"Still, that's sad. I'm sorry that happened to you."

She shakes her head. "There's no reason to be sorry." Sitting at the table, she motions for me to do the same. "I want to tell you a secret," she says.

I nod solemnly.

"I'm running away."

"That's . . . wow. Are you sure? That seems—" I search for the word. "Dangerous," I finish.

"It's not. I have someone helping me."

"Your sister?" I ask.

"Not exactly. I haven't been entirely honest with you, Sam. My sister is the person I've told you about. Lissa is smart, and kind, and beautiful, and talented. Lissa also has . . ." She pauses, looking at the table. "Problems."

"What kind of problems?"

"Drug problems. She moved to New York City and was an actress for a while. She doesn't act much anymore, though. With the way things are, my parents have cut ties with her. They've tried to make me cut ties too. No calls. No letters. It's been . . ." She trails off, looking into the distance. "Hard."

"Ashley, that's terrible. Your parents—I don't understand. Melissa is still their daughter?" I say it almost as a question.

"They don't see it that way. I don't know why. It was a long couple years, watching her life fall apart. Then my parents decided I couldn't contact her, either. They said she was a 'bad influence,'" she says, putting the phrase in air quotes. "I've found ways to contact her occasionally—that's why I was grounded on Friday. I tried to call her, and they found out. Still, it's not the same. It's not enough.

"I said it's been hard, but in truth—it's been unbearable. I decided to do something about it. I've been meaning for weeks to run, but there was never a chance," she says, voice catching with emotion. "If I could, I'd bring the money with me. That morning with you and the dog, I finally had my opportunity. Then later, when I took the money, it was like it was meant to be. My sister's friend from high school lives an hour from here; she's picking me up to take me to Morgantown. There, I'll catch a bus to Pittsburgh, and then on to New York City. That's the plan."

"And once you get to New York? What then?"

"Find Melissa. Help her. Other than that, I don't know."

"The Lord will provide, right?"

I mean it as a joke, but she nods solemnly.

With nothing else to do, I take a few moments to comb my fingers through my hair. Finally, I manage, "Wow. I . . . Ashley, I don't know what to say to that. I'm sorry you feel this is your only solution. Melissa is lucky to have a sister who cares as much as you do. I can't imagine the situation you're in. And, with your parents too. Like I said, I don't know *what* to say."

"Say you wish me luck."

"I *do* wish you luck."

The lights from the Big6 illuminate the area in soft tones. Ashley appears to be holding back tears, and I can understand why. I clear my throat and run my fingers through my hair again, the nervous habit I can't break. "Parents, huh. I have a secret too."

Ashley looks up at me, eyes calm, waiting.

"I, uh . . . I think my dad is dead."

As her eyes widen in shock, I quickly add, "It's okay, it happened a long time ago. Or, well—I mean, it happens tonight . . ." I trail off. I think about how my dad has never come home on a Sunday, this Sunday.

I think he can't come home. I think he's dead. I think he's wrapped around a tree on the side of a road somewhere. Or dead of a heart attack, sitting right there at a blackjack table. Dead at the bottom of a flight of stairs that were a little too steep, or because of a million other reasons that don't matter since the outcome is still the same. But I don't say any of that.

"It doesn't make a lot of sense. Let me start over." I think for a second. "My dad is—no, *was*. He *was* not a good person. I think he was a bad cop, and an even worse father. My birthday was Thursday—you know that, I don't know why I'm telling you again. My mom's whole side of the family . . . well, they don't like my dad, and Dad doesn't let Mom talk to them, but they still send me cards every year for my birthday, all my aunts and uncles and grandparents. Well, he took the money from my birthday cards and was using it to gamble at the casino." I catch Ashley's look and wave it away. "He does it every year, it's nothing new," I explain. "He was supposed to be back tonight, but he's late. And I don't think he's coming back. Ever."

"Why do you think that?" she manages.

I smile sadly. "That's complicated. It's not a story that will make any sense. Remember what I said earlier, about bad luck?" Ashley nods. "I think some people get on the cosmic hook for reasons they don't deserve. And I think that's what's happened to me. I think all my dad's failures, his problems, his everything . . . I think they're my responsibility now."

"Sam, that doesn't make sense."

"It doesn't have to make sense. It just . . . is."

I don't tell her the worst part, I can't. Can't bring myself to tell her that—I don't feel *bad* about it. No anger. No sadness. Just—nothing, a big black pit where a heart should be. *Bad duck*, I think.

There's a moment before Ashley speaks. "I am so very, very sorry. I may not understand, but you're right. I don't have to. No one can tell you how to grieve." She takes my hand in hers and squeezes it. "Two bad ducks."

Smiling ruefully, I echo, "Two bad ducks."

Ashley looks at me. "Come to New York. We could start over. We have the money. I think—" She pauses, choosing her next words carefully. "I think there's nothing left here for you."

Bitterly, I smile. "I can't do that, Ashley."

"Why not? You're eighteen now, you could leave. Didn't you sign your name on the rock? Don't you look at the stars and want something more? This is your chance. Come to New York with me. Forget this place. Start over."

"I . . . I can't, Ashley. I wish I could, but I have things here I need to do."

"Things? Things more important than starting a life, a real life?" A bit of an accusatory tone has leaked into her voice.

I pull my hand from hers. "Like I said, it—it doesn't make sense. I need to stay here. I'm sorry. I wish I could go. I *want* to go." *You can't possibly know how much I want it,* I think. "But I can't leave."

Ashley smiles sadly. "The only person making you stay is yourself." She sighs. "If I'm honest, I didn't think you'd accept my offer. But that doesn't mean I don't wish you'd reconsider."

She pulls open her backpack and flips back the cover of a well-worn notebook, rifling through the pages before tearing one out. "I wrote this for you. It's a poem. I hope you like it."

I take the page, but in the dark I can't quite make out the dense, slanted words. "Thanks, Ashley," I say, voice husky.

"Call me tomorrow when I get to the city. This is my sister's number; she doesn't always pick up, but I will." She scribbles the digits onto a corner of a piece of paper and tears it out. I take it from her and put it in my pocket.

Just then, a beaten-up old sedan pulls into the lot. It honks once. "That must be my sister's friend."

Ashley zips up her backpack and shoulders it, taking a step back uncertainly. "You're sure you won't come?" she asks a final time.

When I shake my head, she smiles sadly. "Okay. Then call me. Please." Stepping forward, she leans up, planting a kiss on my cheek.

I touch my hand to my face, stunned.

"Thank you, Sam Riley. For everything." She walks to the car, opening the door slightly before turning back to me. "Again, I'm—I'm sorry about your dad. No matter the kind of person he may have been, it's not fair for you to have to go through this."

"Thanks," I tell her, because I don't know what else to say.

"And . . ." She hesitates for a moment, then says all in a rush, "I didn't say it before, but I'm also sorry about what happened to Andy. I didn't know him well, but he was always kind to me."

I take a step back, like I've been punched.

With that, she gives me a sad, small wave, climbs into the car, and is off.

———————

I don't know what to do. I feel numb. There isn't a single thought in my head. It feels like every one of my senses has been drowned, like there's nothing left of me but an empty shell.

Stumbling over to the gas pumps where the lighting is better, I pull open the poem Ashley had left to me. "Our Moths," it's titled, the text scrawled across the top of the page.

Sometimes I think I lie a lot,
though I wish I wouldn't,
since when I lie it's to myself,
although I know I shouldn't.

If sins of mine are monsters, my lies are fragile little moths.
They alight soft upon my body, I can't bring myself to brush
them off.

"I am fine." Gently, another moth will land.
"I'm all right," I tell myself, the charade that never ends.

How many lies can I tell before I am a liar?
How many moths can come to rest till I begin to tire?

I miss my limbs unadorned, but can't bring myself to stop.
People say they want the truth, but no, they only want a moth.

A drop of liquid falls onto the sheet, and I realize I'm crying. I take the page and fold it, placing in my pocket. I slide down the side of the pump I'm leaning on, put my head between my knees, and cry like the world is ending, and I'm the only one who knows it.

I think forever passes while I'm sitting like that, broken inside and feeling nothing but a ball of hurt that presses, presses heavily on my lungs and on my stomach and isn't ever going to let up, ever. Finally, even that begins to subside, and I slowly pull some semblance of consciousness out of the black pit of hurt that gapes in my gut.

Wiping my tears, I absently wonder what my dad would say if he saw me like this. I realize it doesn't matter. Nothing matters. It'll be tomorrow in a few hours, and I'll live the same thing over again. Except it won't really *be* the same, now that I know I have the ability to be happy, truly happy—but also the knowledge that it can't last. *Bad duck,* I think.

I stay like that for a while, miserable and wracked, before I'm blinded by a set of sweeping car lights. A car parks next to me, and Mom gets out.

"Samuel!" she cries. "Do you have any idea how long I've been looking for you?" I don't answer. She stops, seeming to register my state. "Are you okay? Have you been hurt? What are you doing out here?" she asks, the edge of hysteria in her voice receding, replaced by an edge of concern.

Still, I don't say anything—I stand, and shove my bike into the back seat of the car and sit in the passenger side, slumped against the door. Mom continues to talk.

"It was late, and you didn't come home, I had no idea where you'd gone. I called Shanna's house, they hadn't seen you. I didn't know what to do, so I called Peety, who told me you might be at the Big6, but he wouldn't say why." She's talking quickly, frantically. "Sam, you need to tell me what is going *on* with you." As we pull out of the station, she starts to cry. "Is it that girl? Are you in trouble? I *knew* that family was bad news—"

I didn't think I had anything left in me, but I snap.

"*That* family is bad news, Mom? You're such a hypocrite. We're not even a family! Dad is horrible at *best*, and you're barely a human around him. I hate him, and I hate you for staying."

Mom slams on the brakes, and the car screeches to a halt in the middle of the empty, moonlit road. Whirling to look at me, she says, "Despite what you may think of me, I am your mother. When your father gets home—"

"When he gets *home*? He's not coming home, is he?" Mom sits back, stunned. "He was supposed to be back *hours* ago, wasn't he? But he never did come back, and you haven't heard from him. You know what I think? I think he's on the side of a road in a *ditch* somewhere"— I'm screaming, my voice cracking—"and you know what else I think? I think he deserves it, Mom. I think he *deserves it!*"

There's a moment of quiet in the car—a long, stunned moment where the world feels like a sheet of ice that's beginning to crack in the middle, and it's not long before the whole thing comes down in shards.

Mom leans forward and puts her hand on my arm.

"Sam, you don't mean that," she says quietly.

Looking into her eyes, I murmur, "I do, Mom." I look down at my hands. "I *do* mean it, and that's the worst part."

I get out of the car and slam the door closed behind me.

"Sam, where are you going?" I head into the trees, Mom calling out to me. "Sam, come back!"

I don't listen to her. I know where I am—even in the dark, I know these woods. I know there's a path here that will take me to the Point. Mom continues to yell after me, but I continue to ignore her. Finally, either she gives up or I'm too deep into the woods to hear her any longer.

I storm through the trees, air heavy and the din of the night bugs screaming. The moon illuminates the thin, weaving path I take upward. It's not far of a walk, only a half a mile or so. I check my watch—11:16.

Soon, I come to the point of Stevens Point Lake, high above the water with a sheer cliff below. I hate this lake. I hate this water, I hate these people, this town, this life. *Bad duck.* I hate myself. I hate all the things I've ever done that don't matter—I hate that nothing matters, nothing, that we're all useless specks on the backdrop of existence—but if I'm here living forever in these three days, does that make me a little bit infinite? I hate that too, that of all the things I could ever have to do or that would ever be expected of me, my fate would forever be to make this town the kind of place my dad could never make it.

It doesn't make sense, does it? It's so inanely stupid, that my fortune and my future would be to police the town I've existed in because my father couldn't do it. That's it. That's all. The sins of the father become the responsibility of the son, and why? Some cosmic prank, a joke I'm on the hook for?

Now you know.

That's what I've been doing these endless cycles of Friday to Sunday and back to Friday again. Just doing . . . my best. I'm so sick of it. I'm so tired. Tired of finding lost dogs and glasses, tired of saving things and people, over and over and over again. I've been tired for months, for years, for days, doing my best to atone for something that isn't mine and shouldn't be my future, my past. I'm just tired.

"Is this what you want? Does this make you *happy*? I've done what you wanted, tried to do it," I scream. "I can't—I can't *do* it anymore. I don't understand. Really? My dad dies and I'm just *screwed,* cursed to be a stand-in for a small-town cop, because why? My dad was useless? And now he's dead, and it's my problem? It's *my problem*?" I'm screaming harder now, voice ragged. Picking up a thick branch, I swing it against the rock wall behind me, where it *thuds* satisfactorily.

"*What?*" I continue. "The *Mine closing* wasn't what you fixated on? Ashley's parents, Chrissy *dying*, Peety that one time, *these* aren't *worthy*—" I hit the rock with the branch over and over again, reverberations traveling up my arm and into my head, into my teeth, "*of*—"

Thud

"*your*—"

Thud

"—*time?*" I hurl the branch off the cliff and into the lake below, then turn to the sheer rock face behind me, which stretches up the mountain indomitably. I smack the face with my open palm, hard, stinging the flesh of my hand.

"*No!* Instead, it's *me,* Sam Riley, who you've got a *problem with*—" I'm hitting the rock wall over, and over, and over again. It abrades my flesh, it stings, hurts, throbs through my palm and my knuckles, but I don't care, I don't care, I'm so angry, I could do this for years and years and years if the stupid lake, stupid cliff, stupid town would hear me. "What's your problem, huh? What's your *problem?*" I punch the rock wall again. "*What's your problem?*" I scream.

The rock face doesn't answer. Of course it doesn't. It's dead—it's not *even* dead, it's worse than dead because it was never alive. It's simply a cold, unfeeling thing, the indifferent subject of my anger. It doesn't care about me. It's not able to.

I stop fighting. I don't have any fire left in me. My knuckles throb; I can't move my fingers. Slumping, I put my face in my hands. Even in the dark, I can see they're streaked with blood. I take a deep, uncertain breath. I think I'm going to cry again, but I don't. There's no point.

"Why me?" I ask, to everyone and no one in particular.

"Why me?" I ask again, slowly shuffling to the cliff, the cliff Chrissy jumped from every Friday before I started telling her dad to watch out for her. It doesn't kill everyone; before Chrissy, the last person who died was a few years ago. It only takes the people who hit the rocks, but I sure hope it'll kill me tonight.

I stand on the precipice, looking over the edge at the ripples in the water that reflects the moon like an expansive, inviting mirror. The warm air blows on all sides of me, ruffling my hair and caressing my face. The stars are out tonight. I speak the first thing that comes to mind.

"I'm sorry," I say, as I let gravity take me over the edge.

SUNDAY, PART 2

It's loud, louder than I thought it would be, as I whistle through the air and crash unceremoniously through the surface of the water. It's dark in the below, and uncomfortably warm. I think about holding my breath and never coming up, but I don't have the fortitude.

Instinctively, I know which way is toward the surface. I claw my way upward, gasping as I breach mere yards from a thin strip of sandy shore. I swim to it, clothing heavy and body exhausted. Collapsing to the rocky beach, I lie on my back, gasping, water stinging my eyes as I stare up at the stars. There's a knot in my stomach. I feel anxious and guilty and scared, all at the same time. I screw my eyes shut, hard, and take a shaky breath. I hear it.

I hear it.

I hear it.

I hear the small voice that's been inside me for this last who knows how long—the one that speaks to me and I don't listen, don't want to listen, *can't* listen.

Bad duck, it whispers to me. *Bad duck. Bad duck, bad duck, bad duck.* The voice tells me I *do* know the answer to the question, the question I don't want to think about, don't want to acknowledge—because if I acknowledge the question, I have to acknowledge the answer. The question of *why me?*

It's been a long time coming, longer than it should have taken for me to face the truth. Dad is wrong about a lot of things. Most things, maybe. But he is right about this. I am a bad duck.

I lie in the dark on my back. My watch reads 11:48. *Plenty of time*, I think.

———————

I close my eyes. And, for the first time in a long time, I let myself remember.

FRIDAY, A MEMORY THREE MONTHS AND THREE DAYS AGO

The school bell rings, signaling the end to another day of classes. I'm grateful for the sound and grateful for the freedom. It's been a long week, as long as a week can be for a seventeen-year-old, and I'm glad it's finally over.

The doors of the building open like a floodgate. Someone calls my name in the rush of students, and I turn around. It's Mickey.

"Sam!" he yells. "Are you going tomorrow?"

I grin. "Wouldn't miss it," I tell him.

"Good," he says. "Eric is home from college this weekend."

"Yeah?" I ask, surprised. "For the bonfire?"

Mickey laughs. "No, not for the bonfire. This Sunday is my mom's birthday."

"And, what? You're going to be hungover for it?"

He laughs again. "Yeah, probably."

"Just make sure you don't fall asleep in church."

"I'll do my best," Mickey says. Giving me a wave, he turns in the opposite direction.

I make my way to the bike rack, where a group of girls is talking animatedly. One of them eyes me as I walk over—a girl in my class named Elle Latner. "Is it true you got the lowest grade in the class on Wednesday's geometry quiz?" she asks.

Smiling sheepishly, I tell her, "It's not that I did that badly, it's just that everyone else did really well."

"I don't think that's it," another girl, Marie, chimes in. "I got a seventy-two. I wouldn't say that's doing 'really well.'"

"Fair point," I admit.

Elle chimes in again. "You'd better be graduating this year, Sam Riley. I wouldn't want to miss you walking across the stage."

"I cross my heart, hope to die, pinkie promise that I will be graduating."

"I'll hold you to that," Elle says. "See you Saturday?"

"Yeah, see you then," I tell her. The group of girls waves to me as I start off on my bike.

It's a Friday afternoon in early March. The air still has a nip to it in the mornings and evenings, but it's past four now and just about comfortable. I've got time before dinner, so I decide to drop by the Big6.

A while later, I pull up in front of the building. Inside, Peety is busy helping the line of people waiting at the counter. I recognize Johnny, the last person in line, and say hi. "What're you here for?" I ask.

"Filling up my dad's car." Johnny motions to a kid standing next to him, a boy maybe thirteen years old who I don't recognize. "This is Zach, my younger brother."

"Nice to meet you, Zach," I say. "I'm Sam."

Looking up at Johnny, Zach asks, "Sam? From the bonfires?"

Johnny looks around warily and smacks his brother lightly on the top of the head. "Keep quiet, Zach. You're gonna get us in trouble."

I grin widely. "Bonfires and other things. In a few years, you can come out and join us."

Zach frowns. "You'll be too old by then. You won't be fun anymore," he says.

I laugh. "We'll see about that."

Johnny puts cash on his pump, and I wave him and his brother goodbye as I lean on the counter in front of Peety. "Busy afternoon," I remark.

Peety snorts. "I wish every day was this busy. What's got that kid talking about bonfires, anyways?"

"Ah, you know how kids talk," I say absently.

Peety arches an eyebrow. "That's all? It's just talk?"

"Now that the weather is a little nicer, we're getting together tomorrow night. Beers. Bonfire." I shrug. "The usual."

"I thought we adults weren't supposed to know about the happenings of the teens in this town?"

"It's basically an open secret. Plus, I know you're too old to hike out and try to bust us."

"You've got me there," Peety says. "Too old for most things, these days."

"That's not true," I tell him. "You're still running this fine establishment. That's no small feat."

Smiling ruefully, he tells me, "Flattery is just lyin' with a little sugar on the top. You had better watch your mouth, Sam Riley, or one day it's going to get you into trouble."

Now it's my turn to smile ruefully. "I'll be lucky if it's my mouth that does that," I tell him. I check my watch. It's almost time to head home, so I say my goodbyes.

"Will you be back tomorrow, before the bonfire?" Peety asks.

"Maybe. I don't know what I'm doing yet."

"If you come by, bring Shanna with you. I haven't seen her in a while," he says, a mischievous twinkle in his eye.

"I'll think about it."

Night is coming in, and the sky is darkening. The air has gotten cooler; there's a brisk edge to the wind as I bike home. Soon the days will be longer and the air warmer, but we're not quite there yet.

I can't wait for summer. *Can't wait, can't wait,* the thought echoes in my mind. Summertime is my favorite time of year. Long days, hot nights, the sounds of the lake and my friends. *And it starts tomorrow,* I think, excited already.

———————

I get home quickly, dropping my bike on the front yard. Then I think about Dad and how much he hates when I do that—the things he'll say about me and my bike if he sees it on the lawn— so I pick it up and set it against the side of the house.

Pushing open the front door, I see Mom busy at work in the kitchen. "What is that? Salad?" I ask, pointing toward a bowl filled with greens.

"It is, and it wouldn't kill you to eat some," she says.

I pretend to consider this. "No, thank you."

She looks me up and down. "You'd better clean yourself up. Your father will be home soon." But it's too late. The lights of his car have already slid past the window and come to rest in the drive. "Well, then," Mom says with a swallow, brushing her fingers on her apron. "Let's sit."

Wordlessly, I plunk myself down in my usual seat at the table. A few long seconds later, Dad opens the door.

Sometimes people tell me I look like him. I hate that. We're both tall, both have brown hair and high cheekbones. Shanna says my eyes are kinder, but I don't know what that means. Dad is in a good mood tonight. We'll see how long it lasts. "Hey, hon," he says to Mom.

Managing a smile, she echoes, "Hey, hon. How was work?"

Dad stretches as he sits down at the head of the table. "New coffee pot broke already—piece of Chinese crap. Rest of the day wasn't better. What's for dinner?"

"Pork chops," Mom says.

"Hmm," Dad says. "They better not be dry. You know how I hate dry pork chops. Like eating a shoe."

Mom doesn't respond to this, just doles them out, one chop per plate. Dad says grace tersely, then cuts into the pork chop and takes a bite, making a face and plunking his knife on the table.

"Lisa, what is this? Leather? Work all day and all a man wants is a good dinner. Is that too much to ask?" Sighing impatiently, he snaps his fingers at Mom. "Ketchup," he orders. She fetches it from the fridge and hands it to him.

"Sorry," she says softly as he grabs it from her.

"If you can't cook a pork chop, don't try to cook a pork chop. It's not difficult." He looks at me. "What's wrong with you? You mute?"

I shake my head no. "Tired. Thinking about school," I lie.

"What's there to think about, huh? You go, you sit for six hours, you come home. That's not hard. Wait till you're out in the real world, working your ass off all day for some leather pork chops," he says, shooting an accusatory glance at Mom, who looks down at the table quickly. Turning back to me, Dad adds, "And take a shower every once in a while, won't you? You smell like a farm." He looks me up and down. "You look like one too."

The rest of dinner passes uneventfully. Dad talks about work—how everyone is an idiot, how nothing is ever done right—and it's just like every other day of walking on eggshells.

Finally, dinner is over, and I excuse myself. "I've got homework," I say.

"Better get that math grade up, Ducky," Dad yells to me as I ascend the stairs.

I don't say anything, just lock myself in my room and open my textbooks. I do my English and my history. I try to do my geometry, but I don't understand it. I don't have more than a halfhearted attempt left in me anyway, so I give up quickly and put my textbooks away, turning on my TV and flipping through the channels.

It's about seven o'clock when I hear a noise coming from my backpack. It's the static buzz of my radio.

"Sam, copy. Sam," a voice crackles. It's the voice I hear sometimes, when I let it slip through the cracks of my mind.

FRIDAY

It's 6:58 a.m., and my eyes open like clockwork. Today is different, though. I feel ill, a kind of deep-seated soul sickness, like my roots are bad.

No Baxter, no Chrissy, no kid with the candy bar at the hardware store for me today. This Friday is for something different.

Feeling miserable and tired, I lie in bed, unmoving. I feel something else too, but can't quite put my finger on it. *I'm nervous*, I realize. I stay like that for a while before Mom knocks on my bedroom door.

"Sam? Are you up?" she asks. I don't say anything. She cracks the door open, then opens it wider when she sees me lying on the bed. "What's wrong? Are you sick?"

"Yes," I tell her after a long moment. I am sick, but not in the way she means it.

Perching on the side of the bed, she asks, "Does your stomach hurt?"

"Everything hurts," I tell her. It's not a lie—not exactly.

"I'll get the thermometer," she says, heading to the bathroom to rifle through the vanity. She returns and sticks it under my tongue. Once it beeps, she pulls it from my mouth and frowns in confusion. "It says you don't have a fever. Are you feeling well enough to go to school?" I shake my head no.

"Your dad isn't going to like this," she says, looking nervously over her shoulder as if he can hear her.

"He doesn't like anything," I tell her, voice emotionless.

"Sam! Don't talk like that about your father."

I don't respond. Mom sits for a long moment, considering. "All right. I'll call the school and let them know you'll be staying home today. Rest up and focus on getting better. Do you want breakfast?" I tell her I don't, and she says she'll be back up later to check on me.

I lie in bed and let the thoughts wash me away.

FRIDAY NIGHT, A MEMORY THREE MONTHS AGO

I fish the radio from my backpack. "Sam here. What's going on?"

"*Checking in. Sorry I couldn't hang after school,*" the voice on the other end crackles.

"No worries. How was the dance recital?" I ask.

There's a lengthy pause. "*Long, Sam, it was long. Two hours and Bella wasn't even on stage for most of it.*"

I laugh. "That's cruel and unusual punishment."

"*It sure was unusual. Any dance you can get a six-year-old to do is going to be interpretive, at best. It's probably for your own good you didn't accept the invite to tag along. I don't think it was your scene.*"

Chuckling again, I reply, "Yeah, and you make it sound like so much fun I probably won't be going to the next one, either."

"*I don't blame you. Hey, I know it's late, but do you want to come over? We've been playing Monopoly, but we're taking a break right now,*" the voice continues. "*We went out for dinner after the recital since Uncle Marvin is in town. I know he'd like to see you.*"

I think about my dad, who is downstairs watching TV. "That's okay. Dad is home, so I probably shouldn't leave the house tonight."

"*Okay,*" the voice says, disappointed. "*I'll tell Uncle Marvin you say hi.*"

"I'm still going to see you tomorrow, right?" I ask.

"*First bonfire of the year? I wouldn't miss it.*"

I smile. "That's what I like to hear. Good luck with Monopoly."

"*Thanks. I need it. See you tomorrow,*" the voice buzzes.

"Yeah. See you tomorrow," I respond.

I put the radio on the windowsill. A while later, I go to bed. Another uneventful Friday night.

FRIDAY

Mom can't help but fret when I'm sick. She gets this way some-times, anxious and pacing, flitting in and out of my room. By now, I'm feeling a bit better, but not by much. There's still a knot in my stomach. I close my eyes and imagine it as a gnarled tree root, alive inside me.

She comes to the door again, leaning inside my room. "I'm sorry, Sam. I have to go out for a little while. I need to run to Bronner—I have to go to the bank, they'll be closed over the weekend." Shifting from foot to foot, she asks, "Will you be all right if I leave you alone for a few hours?"

"I'll be okay. I'm feeling a little better now, actually," I say.

Relief washes over Mom's face. "I'm glad to hear that. Not much of a gift, huh? Coming down with something the day after your birthday?"

"Happy birthday to me," I say ruefully. Mom sits on the edge of my bed and sets the back of her hand against my fore-head, feeling to see if I'm hot.

"You still don't feel warm, which is good. Are you sure you'll be all right if I leave for a bit?" she asks.

I nod. "I'll be fine. Go to Bronner."

"Okay," she says. "But I won't be gone long. There's canned soup in the pantry if you're feeling good enough to eat some lunch. All you need to do is microwave it."

"I know, Mom. I know how to make soup."

"Sorry. I know you do." She gets up to leave. "I'll be back soon," she says, and closes the door softly behind her.

I wait until I hear her leave the house; then I get out of bed and make myself get dressed. *Jeans on, shirt on,* I think to myself, stomach churning.

Forcing myself to brush my teeth, I look at my reflection in the bathroom mirror. Same hair, same face, same eyes, a little more dazed than usual, maybe. I splash water on my face and look at myself again.

Do you recognize them? The changes that happen day by day, etched into your face and your body over time? The lines of life that play out over your forehead and your cheeks, or the freckles on your nose as they appear in the summer and fade in the winter? I don't think you do. I look in the mirror at the same face I've seen my whole life and then some, and I still don't recognize it.

Suddenly, I smack the mirror hard, with an open palm. It leaves behind a wet handprint on the glass. The person staring back at me doesn't flinch.

I gather up my water bottle and my things, then head outside. Picking up my bike, I pedal towards Stevens Point Lake.

It's past noon already. I'm never around at this time of day, always in school, so the life I see surprises me. Neighbors are mowing their lawns. Young kids in yards are tossing balls, and dogs bark at me as I pedal along, a stranger with the audacity to occupy the space in front of their house. It feels wrong somehow. *It feels*, I think, as a vocabulary word from my English class bubbles to the front of my mind—*anachronistic*. Something out of place or time. Mr. Peters would be proud.

The green of the grass and the trees and the gray of the asphalt stretches on, on, endlessly, until I've reached my destination, the same place I was last night: the woods by Stevens Point. I look into the trees, which wave gently in the wind, dappling sunlight through their boughs. I stop for a moment to feel the sunshine on my skin and hear the rustling of the leaves and the song of the birds. Somewhere out of sight, a car engine rumbles. *It's peaceful,* I think, trying to quiet the storm in my head and in my stomach.

I head into the woods, in the opposite direction of where I went the night before. I leave my bike lying on its side on the ground along the trailhead.

"*Are you really going to bring that in here?*" the voice asks. It's a memory again, but I don't force it away this time.

"It's way faster," I say.

"*It rained last night. The trails will be mud.*"

"You think so? Only one way to find out."

I refocus. I could bring my bike—the trails are dry today—but I don't want to. It wouldn't feel right.

The woods are brimming with life—dragonflies, spiderwebs, gnats that fly into my eyes and get stuck in my sweat. A fly buzzes into my ear, forcing me to duck instinctively.

"*They like you!*" the voice says.

"I wish they didn't."

It's about a mile to the bonfire site, but it feels like a hundred. I'm tired, so tired—mentally, emotionally, exhausted. The knot is still there in my gut, dense and heavy. I keep walking.

Finally, I come upon the clearing. I'm not ready to do this yet, so I strip off my socks and shoes and wander into the water up to my shins. I find a smooth pebble and try to skip it across the surface of the lake, but it sinks almost immediately.

"*Wow. Eighteen years on this planet and you still can't throw a rock,*" the voice nags gently.

I comb my fingers through my hair. It's time. Putting my shoes back on, I make the slow walk to Name Rock.

I look at the spot where Ashley signed her name. Of course, it isn't there anymore. *It never happened,* I think, as the sadness pangs in my gut. I look for my name, finding it, the small "Sam Riley" I etched into the face months ago. I realize now that I never should have put it there. I don't deserve to be on the rock with my peers, but still, there I am. *Forever,* I think. Funny how these things happen—how those who don't deserve things can have them while the deserving go without.

I look at the other names too. Most I don't recognize, but some I do. I see Shanna's name, my fingers tracing the letters. I find Johnny, who I haven't spoken to in weeks but whose smile used to brighten all my classes. I find Elle, who loves to talk, and Chrissy, whose tragic death is going to happen tonight because today I didn't prevent it. *Bad duck,* the voice whispers.

Fishing a small Swiss Army knife from my backpack, I lean my forehead against the rock. The sight of the knife makes me sick; I wish the rock would open up and swallow me whole, would turn me into stone so I never have to feel anything, ever again.

Then, I force myself to stand upright and add a new name to the rock. *The* name. The only name that's ever mattered, and the one I've tried every day to forget.

ANDY MAYR, it reads.

I sit on the ground and bury my face in my hands. Slowly, I tip over and lie in the dirt, the only place I belong.

SATURDAY, A MEMORY THREE MONTHS AGO

I wake up late, my breath smelling like the stale chips I pilfered from the pantry as a midnight snack the night before. My alarm clock says it's ten forty, and my bones hurt in the way that only happens when you don't move for too long. After a satisfying stretch, I get dressed.

Mom is downstairs, cooking an egg on the stovetop. We have these ancient nonstick pans she swears will give us cancer, but she never asks Dad for new ones. "Morning. You want an egg?" she offers. She seems tired.

"From the cancer pan?" I ask. "I'll stick with toast."

Mom doesn't think that's funny. Aloud, though, she simply asks, "You have plans for today?"

"I'm going to Bronner with Andy tonight. We're seeing a midnight showing of *Hunting the Werewolf II*, so I won't be home until late."

Mom raises an eyebrow. "Are you sure that's what you're doing? And if I call Mrs. Mayr, she'll tell me she's driving you?"

Bristling uncomfortably, I say, "I mean, yeah." I'm a bad liar.

Mom hands me a plate for my toast. "You stay out of trouble," she says, but that's the last she mentions it.

I eat half a loaf of bread for breakfast, turning slices into toast and buttering them generously as Mom picks up the kitchen. She looks at me I put my plate in the dishwasher and says absently, "I'm going to have to go grocery shopping again."

"I'm going to Andy's," I tell her. She waves at me as I head outside. The day is cool; I'm glad I wore a hoodie.

I pedal north. Not many people are about, but I wave to the ones that are. Mrs. Dean flags me down as I coast in front of her driveway. I skid to a stop in front of her.

"You really ought to wear a helmet," she admonishes, double chin waggling up and down as she speaks.

"I know, Mrs. Dean. But helmets give me helmet hair, and if the girls see me like that, I'll never get a date to prom." She smiles.

"Something tells me you won't ever have that problem. Say, will you mow my grass again this year? It's chilly now, but it'll be warm again before we know it."

"Of course, Mrs. Dean. Just let me know when you need help." She thanks me and waves me off, saying she'll phone the house when she wants me over.

Eventually, I slow in front of a brick house with green louvers. A split-level, Mom would call it. It's a little different than most of the houses in the neighborhood, but I like it. It's got an air of warmth to it, a sense of welcome that's hard to put your finger on. I drop my bike in the lawn and knock on the front door. "JESUS LOVES YOU" reads a small sign in an Easter-themed wreath that's hung on the door at eye level. *Easter isn't for another month,* I think, as a little girl opens the door and grins up at me.

"Tham," she says, butchering the *S,* "whath the pathword?"

"Please," I tell her.

"Thath not the pathword," she says stubbornly.

"I'm pretty sure that's always the password." She pouts at me, and I change the subject. "I heard you had a great dance recital last night."

At this, she beams, again revealing the missing front tooth that's the culprit of her lisp. "I did. I wore my dreth and I got to danth and then everyone thaid I did *great.*"

"I believe it. In fact, I bet you did the best job anyone has ever done at dancing. Now, can you please let me in so I can see your brother?"

She opens the door, but she isn't happy about it. "I don't know why you want to thee him. He doethn't like danthing."

"I'll tell him you said that."

I make my way into a small foyer, where can I hear the clattering of pots and pans coming from upstairs. A woman appears at the top of the short flight of steps. "Hi, Mrs. Mayr," I call up to her. "I saw your wreath. It's a bit early for Easter decorations, isn't it?"

"I like to be prepared. Speaking of preparing things, you're here right on time to help me open this jar," she says, and waves me up to her. She's a short woman with copper hair, bright green eyes, and an apron that's covered in flour. "Bella and I made pasta from scratch for lunch. I was planning on making the sauce from scratch too, but I'm just too tired. I've been cooking, and Bella has been—" She eyes the kitchen, where it looks like a small flour-filled bomb has gone off. "Well, Bella has been throwing flour around, mostly." Bella giggles and claps her hands over her mouth.

"That's why I never let my kids in the kitchen," I say, popping the jar of pasta sauce open and handing it back to her.

"No joking about that, Sam. No having kids till you're married and at least thirty-five years old," she admonishes.

I smile.

"Believe me, Mrs. Mayr, you do not have to worry about that."

"Good!" she exclaims. "You'd better keep it that way." She pours the sauce from the jar into a pan on the stove. "Andy is still sleeping. Andy! *ANDY!*" she yells, then looks at me with a bright smile. "He's probably not sleeping anymore. Go get him, please. It's time for lunch. Are you hungry?"

"I ate half a loaf of bread for breakfast."

"Just the bread?"

"I put butter on it."

"You know, there are other ways you can eat bread. Sandwiches, melts, peanut butter and jelly. You don't have to eat it plain."

I wave her off. "I like my bread boring. I'll go get Andy."

I make my way to a small bedroom off the living room in the downstairs level. I knock on the door, and a lethargic voice answers me. "What?"

I crack the door open. "Wakey-wakey," I say, dodging a pillow that's chucked at me halfheartedly. Andy is lying in bed, so I sit on the chair at his desk.

I've known Andy for as long as I can remember. I can't recall exactly how we met, and he can't either. My first memory is of kicking a soccer ball with him at recess in second grade. My second memory is of me then tripping and falling, scraping my knee and Andy getting a teacher to give me a cartoon-themed Band-Aid to patch me up.

Andy and I have always been inseparable, have always been there for each other. We do most everything together—play baseball, ride our bikes, do our homework, and do nothing together, absolutely nothing at all. We're closer than most brothers, and I wouldn't trade him for the world.

When I tell him it's lunchtime, he sits up quickly. "Already?" he asks.

Smiling, I reply, "Time flies when you're dead to the world."

He gets out of bed and pulls on a T-shirt, top half ready for the day but bottom half still pajamaed. "What's for lunch? I'm starving."

"Pasta," I tell him.

He frowns. "I thought pasta was more of a dinner dish."

I consider the mess upstairs. "I think it's more of a science experiment than anything else."

Andy scratches his nose. "I don't know if I'm so hungry anymore," he says, but heads upstairs anyway.

"Look at the sleepyhead, finally awake," Mrs. Mayr says as we make our way into the kitchen. "People who don't cook—"

"Do dishes, I know," Andy finishes his mom's thought, eying the mess around him. "Do they also clean countertops?" he asks, then looks down. "And floors?"

Mrs. Mayr laughs. "I'll help with that. And so will Bella," she says pointedly to her little girl, who's drawing with crayons at the table.

"Noooooooooo," Bella pouts.

"Yes, missy messy, you'll be helping to clean too," Mrs. Mayr says. "Lunch is almost ready—please put the plates out." Andy and I set the table as she doles out pasta. The noodles are irregularly sized but quite delicious.

Over lunch, we talk about a little bit of everything—how the weather is starting to warm, what's going on at school. Bella regales us with her tale of last night's dance recital, an exciting spectacle with lots of jumping and prancing. I glance at Andy, who rolls his eyes good-naturedly.

After lunch, Andy gets dressed and we pick up the plates. Together, we wipe the counters and sweep flour off the floor. Then we make our way back to his bedroom, where he has an old gaming system hooked up to a small TV in the corner. "What're we feeling?" he asks.

We end up playing a racing game. It's an old console and an old game, where the cars are all polygons with weird boxy angles everywhere. Andy's much better at the game than I am; he beats me handily four races in a row. After the fourth win, he puts down his controller.

"I can't wait to have my own car," he says wistfully.

I snort. "You and everybody else. What I can't figure out is what you plan to do with it. *Having* a car doesn't mean you've got anywhere to go."

Andy considers this for a moment. "I think it's less about the going, and more about the being able to go," he says quietly.

For some reason, this makes me uncomfortable, so I brush over it. "The problem with driving is that you're not supposed to drink and do it. No one cares if you're buzzed on a bicycle," I say wisely.

Andy smiles. "I think you'd have more of a problem with that than I do."

I pretend to be offended. "And what does *that* mean? You calling me a drunk, Andy Mayr?"

Smirking, he replies, "I would never. But *speaking* of having problems, what happened with that geometry quiz Wednesday? You told me you studied."

I grin sheepishly. "Well, I really was going to study. And then, the craziest thing happened. I didn't."

"Sam," he says, his smile sliding into something like disappointment. "If you keep this up, you're going to fail."

"Yeah, and would that be so bad?" I ask. "I don't know why you're so eager to get out of here, anyway. I could do another year of this."

"Stop trying to change the subject. If you fail one class, you probably won't need to repeat the grade. Instead you'll have to go to summer school or to Bronner every day to take classes at the community college. Is that what you want?" Andy asks.

I sigh. He's been so eager to *lecture* me lately. "I *know,* Andy. I'm just so bad at math."

"Hey, no excuses," he interjects. "You're not bad at math, you're bad at buckling down. And I've got a surprise for you." He goes to his backpack.

"No. No, no, no, no, noooooooooooo," I plead as he pulls his geometry textbook from his backpack. "It's the *weekend,* Andy. Saturdays are *sacred*. Doesn't that mean anything to you?"

"The weekend is the time you have to do to everything you didn't get around to doing during the week. For example, studying geometry."

I groan, but he's already flipping through the pages. "Please don't make me do this," I beg.

He looks at me. "How about we make a deal? If we study for one hour, I'll ask Mom if you can stay for dinner. My aunt brought a pie yesterday. There's some left over, and if you study with me, you can have it for dessert."

I give Andy a shrewd look. "What kind of pie?"

"Blueberry," he says. "Homemade crust and all."

"That's not fair!" I say, exasperated. "You *know* that's my favorite."

We study for an hour, the shapes and angles making more sense now than they did when we began. "Do you think you'll be ready for next week's quiz?" Andy asks.

I shrug. "Depends on what we learn next week and if any of it makes sense."

"Then we'll have to do this again on Tuesday," he says.

"Only if your aunt is making another pie you can bribe me with."

Andy smiles. "I'm sure we can think of something."

The studying over with, we find an early nineties action movie on TV. As we watch it, we poke fun at the bad special effects and over-the-top gun fights. "Why are you so tired today, anyway?" I ask during a lull in the carnage. "You're usually a morning person."

"I stayed up too late reading a book," Andy replies.

I arch an eyebrow. "The sci-fi one?"

"Same series, different book. There are seven of them."

"You'd better learn to read during the day," I tell him. "You're never going to get to sleep if you keep up this space stuff."

"I know. It's my fault. I lost track of time, and suddenly it was three in the morning."

"Why do you like these books so much, anyway?" I ask him, picking up a thick novel off the floor at the foot of his bed. It's an old paperback, the cover displaying an embossed picture of a man and his alien companion on a fictional planet. The duo stands confidently in front of a skyline of futuristic skyscrapers and spaceships on the horizon.

Andy sees me looking at it. "That's the first book. You can borrow it if you want."

Snorting, I tell him, "I'll wait for the movie to come out, thanks. Besides, you didn't answer my question."

"They're good books. There's action, and mystery, and I like the 'space stuff.'"

"Humans are never going to get off this planet," I say. "And even if we did, it doesn't matter. There's nothing else out there."

"Humanity is never going to get off this planet or find anything else, *if* everyone keeps thinking like that," he tells me, taking the book from my hands and looking at it himself. "And if we could get out there, and if we did find something, wouldn't that be incredible?"

"So what? You're going to be an astronaut now?" I ask. Andy shrugs. "Big dreams lead to big disappointment," I tell him.

"What then? It's better to have no goals and never dream of anything?"

I'm about to respond when Mrs. Mayr opens the door. "Are you boys going to be hungry for dinner soon?" she asks.

Andy smiles. "I'm always hungry," he says.

Mrs. Mayr looks at me. "Andy told me you get the rest of the pie."

"That was the deal. Sorry, Mrs. Mayr."

We eat a short while later. Andy's dad is still on the road, so it's only the four of us for dinner. Since we covered all the important mealtime conversations over lunch, now we talk just to talk. Mrs. Mayr tells us about the dinners her mother used to make on Saturdays, and how her father usually couldn't eat with the rest of the family because he worked the weekend shift at the Mine. "He got Sunday mornings off for church, but other than that he worked all weekend."

Looking over at Andy, I see he's eyeing me. "Compared to that, I guess a little geometry doesn't seem so bad," I admit.

After Mrs. Mayr has reheated the pie in the oven, I dig into the couple slices that are left. "This is amazing," I tell her—Andy makes a motion to steal a scoop of filling from the tin, but I bat his spoon away with my fork. "Absolutely not," I tell him. "I earned this pie."

Grinning, he goes in a second time with his spoon, anyway. I let him have the bite, rolling my eyes. Finishing all of what's in the tin, I scrape the sides clean with my fork.

"Where does all this food go?" Mrs. Mayr marvels.

"I've no idea," I tell her truthfully, looking at the time. "Crap,

I should get going. I told Shanna I'd stop by tonight before—before the movie."

"The movie, huh?" Mrs. Mayr raises an eyebrow. "I heard you two are going to be out late tonight."

"Yeah . . . pretty late," I tell her.

"Make sure you dress warm. 'Movie theaters' get cold at night this time of year," she says. She knows where we're really headed, but we all still play along.

"Thanks for dinner and thanks for the pie." I turn to Andy. "You'll be at my house at about seven?"

"Yeah," he says, walking to the door with me. "I'll be there at seven. Hey, before you go—" He stops.

"What's that?" I ask. Andy is standing in the doorway, me on the porch.

"It's—nothing. We can talk about it later. It's not important," he says. "I don't want you to be late to Shanna's."

"Yeah? Okay. See you at seven, then," I tell him as I turn around.

"And dress warm!" I hear Mrs. Mayr call out from behind me as Andy closes the front door.

I pull up in front of my house, but I don't go in. Instead, I lean my bike against the front steps and cross the street, knocking on the door of the house kitty-corner from mine. No one answers, so I go around and let myself in through the back door, heading directly down a narrow, steep flight of stairs and into the basement.

It's a small basement, but Shanna's claimed all of it, turning it into a kind of sprawling, oversized bedroom. She's lying on the couch as I come in. My mom would call it a loveseat, a little two-seater in a faded blue pattern. As I make my way down the stairs, Shanna looks up, scooting upright to make room for me to sit. She's cocooned in quilts, the top half of her head sticking out to watch TV. It's chilly in the basement, but not cold.

"You okay? You look rough. What's going on?" I ask, taking a seat by her on the couch.

She leans against me, a spongy mass of fabric. "I don't feel good," she says miserably.

"You weren't in school yesterday, but I didn't know you were this sick," I tell her, concerned.

"Yeah. My stomach feels like a lava lamp, like my insides are moving. And I'm freezing all the time."

"And you wanted me to come over so you can make me sick too?" I ask, but she doesn't appreciate my joke.

"Hang out with me. Mom and Dad are at work."

"Are you hungry?" I ask. Shanna nods. I find crackers and canned soup in the pantry, heating up the soup on the stovetop. "Hope you like cream of mushroom," I tell her as I hand her the bowl, "because it's all I could find."

"Mom uses it for casseroles," she says, eating it slowly with a spoon.

"You're going to miss the bonfire tonight," I tell her.

She groans miserably. "I know. Don't remind me."

As she continues eating, I fill the silence. "I met Johnny's younger brother yesterday at the Big6."

"Zach?" Shanna asks. "I used to babysit him sometimes. He's a cute kid. He used to be really, really into race cars. We'd play with his little car figurines for hours. I hope he's grown out of it."

I think about the boy I met the day before, who seemed to be too old for Hot Wheels now. "I think he has," I assure her. "Also, Mickey's brother is home from college. Mickey said he's coming out tonight."

"He came back for the bonfire?" Shanna asks.

I laugh. "No, but I asked Mickey the same thing. It's their mom's birthday this weekend."

"That's nice," she says, munching on a cracker. "You'll have to tell me about it tomorrow. I'm really bummed I won't make it."

"Yeah," I say. "I am too."

We sit together for a while, watching reruns of old game shows. I don't like game shows all that much; I think they're boring and I always feel bad for the people who don't win. But Shanna is the one who's sick, so she gets to pick the channel. Eventually, I tell her it's time for me to head home.

"Have fun," Shanna says, waving to me miserably as I leave. I tell her I will—but not too much fun, not without her.

Back at my house, I change my jeans and pull on a different hoodie, one without pasta stains. A few seconds later, my radio crackles.

"*Sam, come in. Sam.*"

Grabbing the radio, I respond to Andy's call. "What's up?"

"*I'll be out front in two. Come down and meet me,*" Andy says.

"Will do."

As I head outside, Andy is pulling up. "You ready?" he asks.

"Sure am," I say, picking up my bike and following him. I tell him Shanna is sick and isn't going to make it out tonight.

"That's too bad," Andy says. "I'll stop by tomorrow and check in on her. No one wants to be alone when they're sick."

We pedal in silence, intent on our destination. The sky is quickly turning dark, and there's an edge to the air already.

"I'm getting cold," I say, breaking the silence.

Andy cracks a smile. "You'd better complain about that now, while you still can. Soon it'll be ninety every day and you're going to miss this kind of weather." He frowns. "It is cold. But at least the bonfire will feel nice."

A while later, we pull up to the woods. Off in the distance, a great squawk of birds all take off at once, darkening the sky with their amorphous flock. I watch them as I lean my bike against a tree, Andy tipping his over to the side in the dirt. It's dark by now, getting close to eight o'clock, but we know where we're going and we've both brought flashlights. I fish mine out of the backpack I keep for nights like these, a pack that holds my flashlight, my radio, and a Swiss Army knife for emergencies like opening bottles of beer that aren't screw-offs.

"Do you remember that time when we were out here and you stepped on that thing that screamed? You thought you'd killed a mouse, but it was just a squeaker in an old dog toy?" I ask.

Andy laughs. "I think about that every time I see a dog toy. It scared me so bad I thought I was going to pass out."

"I was surprised you didn't," I tell him, laughing.

"Are you excited?" Andy asks suddenly.

I stop laughing, surprised by his question. "For what? The bonfire? Of course."

"You don't think it's a little sad, though, too?"

I frown, confused. "What do you mean?"

I can't see Andy well in the darkness, but I imagine he shrugs. "You know. It's the beginning of the end," he says.

I'm taken aback. "I guess I hadn't thought about it that way."

"It all has to end someday, right? We won't be out here doing this next year."

"I know that," I say, starting to get irritated.

"I think it's special because it doesn't last forever," Andy continues. Even in the dark, I can feel him looking at me.

"I don't know, Andy. I haven't really been paying attention. I'm trying to not get lost out here."

"You couldn't get lost in these woods if you tried," he says with a laugh.

We walk in silence, the sound of the night creatures echoing as our shoes crunch against the dirt. I'm a little irritated with Andy. I'm just trying to have a good time tonight—I've been waiting for this bonfire for months. Obviously I know high school won't last forever, but that doesn't mean I want to think about it right now.

The sound of the night begins to give way to people talking and laughing, music playing in the background. We come down the hill and see a group of maybe twenty-five people mingling around a huge bonfire burning in the middle of the flat plateau. The fire casts long, red, flickering shadows over the faces of the crowd in the way only flames can. Off to the right, a steep slope leads to a rocky strip of beach and the water. Above the slope is a tree on which is tied a long rope swing, vacant and unused until the summer months come. A few people wave to us as we join the throng of people.

Andy and I say hi to our friends and make small talk. Most of the people here are people we know, but some aren't. I'm sure we'll know them soon, though; that's how these things always seem to work.

We make our way to a keg and a stack of red plastic cups. Warm from the fire, they glint in the light. There's a cup stuffed with bills of different denominations sitting next to the keg. "Is it your turn to pay or mine?" I ask Andy.

He frowns. "I don't know. I can't remember."

"I'll rock-paper-scissors you for it," I offer. When I throw a rock and he throws scissors, I grin. "Good, because I don't have any cash on me."

Rolling his eyes, Andy puts a ten-dollar bill and a couple ones into the cup with the rest of the money. "You'd better bring cash next time," he says, "because I'm going to remember this, and next time you're paying."

"It's a deal," I tell him, and fill a cup with beer from the keg. I pour Andy's cup about a quarter full and hand it to him. As we look around the scene, I point at Elle, who's chatting with another girl back near the tree line. "Elle was making fun of me yesterday for failing that geometry quiz," I tell him.

Andy smacks his palm to his forehead in distress. "Sam! You didn't tell me you'd *failed* it," he says, exasperated.

"Oops," I say, grinning sheepishly into my beer.

"You'll come over tomorrow night and we'll study some more. We can ask Mr. Greenleigh for the sections we'll be covering next week and get a head start on those." He continues, but I've already tuned him out.

A few yards away, I see Mickey with an older guy. *His brother,* I think. I walk over to them, seeing an opportunity to get Andy to stop thinking about school. "Hey, Mickey. Is this your brother?" I motion to the guy by his side.

"Hey, Sam. Yeah, this is Eric."

I shake Eric's hand. "I think we've met before," I tell him, "but it's been a while." Andy has already appeared at my shoulder. "This is Andy."

"Hello," Andy says. "It's nice to meet you. I heard you're home from college?"

"That's right," Eric says. "I'm Mickey's ride tonight. I thought I'd swing by and see how the old spot is doing."

"We keep it clean," Andy says.

"And fun," I tell Eric.

He laughs at this. "I'm sure you do."

"Where do you go to college?" Andy asks.

"Morgantown."

"Wow, that's great. What do you study?"

"Engineering."

Nodding, Andy tells him, "My uncle is an engineer."

As their conversation continues, I turn to Mickey. "What's new with you?" I ask.

Shrugging, he tells me, "Mom's dinner is tomorrow night. My aunt and uncle are coming out for it. She doesn't get along with either of them, so that'll be fun." He rolls his eyes. "My cousins are coming too. They're in elementary school and they scream all the time. It's going to be a rough day."

"It'll be even rougher with a hangover," I tell him.

"This is light beer, I'll be okay. Plus, I've got Eric to get me home, and I'll take an Advil before bed."

"Advil? What does that do?"

"It helps prevent hangovers. Bad for the liver, though, my dad says."

I chat with Mickey a while longer and drink my beer, then get another and chat some more. I start to cycle through a revolving door of people, most familiar faces, but also some I don't know. I meet a girl from Bronner who rides horses and a guy from Virginia—"not West Virginia," as he constantly tells people—who is visiting his mom and stepdad for the weekend. I meet a boy who just moved here in February and has a birthmark on his cheek the size of a dime. I tell him I think it's cool. "You think so?" he asks curiously. "Most people try to ignore it."

I'm about five beers deep when Elle walks over to me. "Hey, Sam," she says. "I would have thought you'd come with Shanna?"

"No Shanna tonight," I tell her. "She's sick."

Elle looks disappointed, but I don't know why. "That's too bad. I hope she feels better."

"Yeah. Me too." I notice she isn't drinking beer like the rest of us. "What's in your cup?"

"Rum and Coke," she says. "I don't like beer."

"Really?" I ask, surprised. "I don't know how anyone could not like beer."

She shrugs. "It makes my stomach hurt and it tastes like bread, but gross."

"I love bread," I say, almost dejectedly.

I'm pretty drunk at this point. I find myself sitting on a log with a sophomore; we're talking about the best and the worst gym units. "Worst is volleyball, best is track," I tell him.

He shakes his head like I'm crazy. "*Worst* is volleyball? Anyone can play volleyball, you're insane. All you do is stand there. Best is badminton and worst is track. They really ask us to run a mile outside at, like, 9:00 a.m., and then come inside and put our clothes on over our gross, sweaty bodies and sit in class all day."

"Best is *badminton*? What are you, English? 'Let me hit the'—the, what is it called? The cone thing? The birdie. 'Let me hit the birdie over this tiny little fence because that's fun, this is fun, badminton is a real sport, I promise,'" I say in a mocking, albeit terrible, English accent.

The guy I'm talking to snorts. "What kind of accent was that?"

"English, can't you tell? 'Because I'm *posh* and I play badminton.'"

"It sounds Australian to me."

Someone taps me on the shoulder. It's Andy. "Hey. How're you doing?" he asks.

"This guy likes badminton," I say, pointing accusatorily at the sophomore sitting next to me.

"I do like badminton," the sophomore says defiantly.

"I do . . . not have much of an opinion on badminton," Andy says. Looking at me, he adds, "You ready to go?"

"Go? Already? I only had three beers," I lie petulantly, "and you need to get your money's worth."

Smiling, Andy replies, "You've had more than that. Besides, it's after midnight. We've been here for more than four hours."

"I don't think so," I say belligerently, but Andy doesn't rise to the bait.

"We've got to go home," he says. "You're drunk."

"And *you're* no fun."

But he's right. It's time, and I know it. The bonfire is dying, and people are loading trash into a garbage can strapped to the back of an ATV. I stand up from the log, and the world spins around me as I sway upright. I realize just how uncoordinated I've become.

"I don't think I'm going to make it home," I say, concerned.

Andy sighs. "Wait here," he tells me, leaving me with the sophomore.

"I can't believe it's midnight already," I tell my younger companion, mostly coherent.

"Time flies when you're trashed," he says.

"What's your name, kid?" I ask him.

"Parker. I've told you three times already. And I'm not a kid."

"Parker, Parker," I say, leaning in close as if I have some great wisdom I'm about to bestow upon him. "We're all kids, because the alternative is worse."

He looks confused. "That we're babies?"

Andy returns. "All right. One of the baseball guys is going to give us a ride to my uncle's shack," he says. "I told him where it is, he can't miss it. He'll take you there and then come back and bring me up. It's only a couple minutes away. We'll get our bikes tomorrow morning."

"What'll my dad say? I'm supposed to be home tonight." The words come out as a slur as Andy loads me onto the back of the ATV.

"If you're lucky, nothing," he replies. "Just hang out till I get there."

The ATV starts up. "Hold on," yells the driver. I try to find something to hold on to, with limited luck. The headlights sear streaks into my retinas, illuminating the forest in front of us as I'm bounced around on the back of the vehicle.

I'm lucky the ride is short. The driver drops me off, a guy I've seen plenty of times before, but I can't pick his name out of the mess that is my brain right now. He asks me if I'll be okay, and I tell him I'll be fine. He says he'll be back with Andy in a few minutes.

My head hurts from the jostling, and my stomach isn't doing so well, either. *I think I'm going to be sick,* I think, just before running off to the side of the shack and vomiting into the underbrush. Wiping my mouth with the back of my hand, I wish I had some water. I do feel better, though I'm not going to tell Andy I've puked. He'd never let me live it down.

Pulling my flashlight from my pocket, I turn it on. The shack is exactly what it sounds like it would be: a place for Andy's uncle to camp out when he's in town fishing. No running water, but it's got a roof and a door and a bunk bed. Andy's uncle doesn't come out here as much as he used to, so it gets most of its use from Andy and me on nights like these. There's a small firepit in front of the shack. I find some mostly dry kindling and sticks, then fetch a lighter from a coffee can under the bunk bed. The kindling ignites, and the fire is cozy. Even with the liquor jacket, I've been getting chilly, so I'm glad to have the warmth.

I pull out two old folding camp chairs from inside the shack. I set them in front of the fire and plop down in one. *I'm tired,* I realize, exhaustion crashing down on me like a wave. I've had a busy day. *A good day,* I think, as I scoot into the chair and make myself comfortable. I'm sobering up quickly now, and I can feel a bit of a headache coming on. I think about Mickey saying "it's only light beer" and wish I had an Advil.

In the distance, I hear the low rumble of the ATV, and soon I see its headlights cutting through the darkness. Andy hops off and gives a hearty thanks to our driver, who raises his hand and wishes us a good night. He then sits down in the camping chair across the fire. "How're you doing?"

I give him two thumbs up. "Feelin' peachy."

"Really? You look pale," he says, then pivots topics. "Too bad Shanna wasn't here tonight."

"Yeah," I say. "I'll have to bring her an Icee from the Big6 tomorrow or something."

"You sobering up?" Andy asks, and I nod. I think about throwing up in the brush.

"The ATV ride helped," I tell him instead. "Now, I'm more tired than anything."

"That's good, I think," he says. For a minute, he disappears into the shack; he comes out with an old bottle of whisky, then unscrews the top and takes a swig, grimacing. "Not great," he tells me, and passes the bottle over.

I frown. This isn't like him.

"You have fun tonight?" he asks, sitting back down.

"I did," I say, putting the bottle on the ground. "Heck of a start to the season. I think I met a bunch of new people, but—" I run my fingers through my hair. "I don't remember much. It's all a blur."

Andy laughs. "Do you remember the girl with the cast?"

I frown. "What cast?"

"The girl with the broken arm, she had a cast. You kept trying to sign it, but you didn't have a pen, so you were trying to sign it with a stick."

"I don't remember that, but it sounds about right," I say with an embarrassed grin.

"Yeah, then she asked you for your number and you kept trying to give her your house number. '502,' you kept saying. 'I live at 502.' Something tells me you're not going to hear from her again," Andy says, breaking into a grin of his own.

I groan. "You could have given her my phone number! You *knew* that was what she wanted," I say, exasperated.

"I can't do that to Shanna. And Elle," he adds.

I groan even louder now, sinking down into my chair and thinking about the conversation I had with Elle earlier. "Crap. I think I blew it with Elle. I'm so oblivious."

Chuckling, Andy replies, "Yeah. Yeah, you really are."

He gets quiet for a moment after that, staring into the fire. "Hey, Sam. I have something to tell you. I wanted to tell you earlier, but we didn't have time."

I laugh. "Is it that Elle has a thing for me? And that I'm an idiot who's going to mess it up at the bonfire?" I'm joking, but when I look up at him, face reflected in the firelight, I can tell he's serious.

"No, Sam. I'm—I'm going to college," he says.

I sit up quickly. "Wait—what? You are? I thought you didn't want to take out loans?"

"I ended up getting a bunch of scholarships," he says, spreading his hands out in front of him. "I'm really lucky. Since I'm only paying for a portion of my tuition, I think I can make it work."

I don't know what to say.

Any friend would be happy for him. *I* should be happy for him. *I am happy for him,* I decide, and do my best to smile.

"That's . . . really amazing, Andy. That's great. You're going to Morgantown?" I ask, feigning enthusiasm. Anyone who goes to college from Redford goes to Morgantown.

"Ah, actually. I'm going to Connecticut."

"*Connecticut?*" I can't help it—it bursts out of me, jumping from my mouth of its own accord. "That's eight states away!" I exclaim.

"I don't think that's exactly how it works—"

"I'm failing geometry, not geography. I know enough about it to know that it's *far.*" *Too far for a bus, and* way *too far to bike,* I think. I want to say more, but I bite my tongue. *I should be happy,* I tell myself. *I am happy,* I tell myself.

"I'm sorry, Sam. There's not a good way to say something like this."

"It's okay. What could you possibly have to be sorry for?" I should stop, I *know* I should stop, but still, I don't. "It couldn't be for telling me, 'Don't worry about it, I'm not going out of state for college, I'll take classes in Bronner and then transfer to Morgantown,' and then going to college in Connecticut, instead."

You're happy for him, I tell myself, but I don't feel happy. I'm starting to feel angry.

"Sam, that *was* the plan. But I applied for acceptance and scholarships anyway, you know that."

"I never thought you'd get anything!"

"I had to try," Andy says, pleading. "I couldn't not try."

I snort. If anyone could pull this off, it would be Andy. *I'm so stupid,* I think. *Bad duck, bad duck. I should have seen this coming.*

"So that's it, then. You're leaving? This summer, and then that's it?" I ask, staring intently into the fire.

"It's not like I'm leaving forever. I'm only going to college."

"Don't say it like that. 'Only going to college,' like it's not four years and four hundred miles away," I say, voice rising.

"I'll be back during the summers—"

"No, you *won't,*" I say bitterly. "You'll get a job in a city. You'll forget about Redford, and you'll never be back."

"That's not true. My family is here, my friends are here—"

"Family and *friends.* Okay, the same family and friends you're leaving for a new life in Boston. Seems like they really mean a lot to you."

"It's not Boston, it's Connecticut—"

"*Fat freaking difference.* It doesn't matter. No one leaves Redford, and the people who do leave *never* come back. We'll just be some hicks from your hometown that you used to know," I say, picking a small stick from the dirt and throwing it angrily into the fire.

"That's not true. And it's not fair, either. I had to do this. It's the right decision for me. Time passes, and—and things change. We're not going to be in high school forever—"

"You keep saying that! I know! I *know* I'm not going to be seventeen forever, I'm not *stupid*. I'm aware of how calendars work, thank you, Mr. Fulbright," I say, sarcastic tone biting. "Just because I'm okay with how things are right now doesn't make me less than you."

"I don't think you're less than me, and I know you're angry—"

"I am angry!" I yell. "I'm angry that you *lied* to me. You *told* me not to worry about it, that you weren't leaving, and here you are. Doing the *one* thing you said you wouldn't."

"It's not that simple—"

"It sure feels that simple. I'm still here, and you're not going to be."

I've been clenching my fists so hard my nails have dug half-moons into my palms. There's a long beat of silence.

"Sam, this could be you too," Andy says quietly, peering at me from across the fire.

"What does that even *mean*?" I ask, exasperated.

"I know you pretend not to care, but I think it's because you've given up. I think you can't see a life for yourself outside this place, so you don't bother trying." Andy is getting angry now too. "I know you can do more with your future than get a job making barbecues in Bronner. I just don't know why you can't see that too!"

"Oh, shut *up,* Andy. Don't *lecture* me. Not all of us have the brains to get into Harvard and 'stellar youth group leadership experience' for our scholarship applications." Outwardly, my voice is mocking, but I'm getting angrier still. Rage burns in my stomach like it's going to eat me from the inside out, so I clench my teeth and my fists even harder to keep it down. "Not all of us have parents who can pay for tuition, even *with* a scholarship. Not all of us have parents who care enough about us to care whether or not we even *apply* for college!"

"You're smart and talented. If you wanted to, you could find a way to make it work."

"Do you know what your problem is? Your problem is that you think everyone is just like you, but that you only work harder." I'm spitting mad, my face growing hot and my ears ringing. "You think everyone is gifted and talented. 'If they would only try a little harder, they could have straight A's and throw the perfect fastball, and have a perfect life with a perfect family.' That's not how it works! That's not how any of this works!"

"Yeah? Well, *your* problem is that you see yourself through your dad's eyes," Andy yells back. "You think you're a bad duck, so that's all you'll ever let yourself be."

I'm stunned. All at once, the anger is gone, replaced by something worse. In this moment, I hate him.

"Don't you say that to me," I tell him quietly. "Don't talk about my dad. That's too much, and you know it." I stand up. "Fuck you, Andy. I hope you die in Connecticut."

Turning my back to the fire, I head out along the path.

"Sam. Sam!" Andy yells after me, at first angry, but then pleading and frustrated. "Come back, Sam, we can talk about it. Sam, I'm sorry. Sam!"

I ignore him, feet pounding purposefully against the dirt in the dark. I fish my flashlight from my backpack and use it to light the way. I can hear the blood rushing in my head. I barely see the path as I stomp along it. Andy shouldn't have said those things about me, about my dad. He doesn't have the right to.

And I'm still angry at him for leaving. It's always been the two of us, from before I can remember. And now what? Just—nothing? I can't believe he'd give it all up, everything, to go to some stupid school in some stupid state I can't even spell.

Bad duck, the voice says. *People let you down, it's what they do.* But I never thought it would be Andy. I thought he cared more than that. I thought I *knew* him better than that.

I finally make my way out of the woods, finding the bikes and pulling mine out from against the tree.

I look at Andy's bike for a long second before shouldering my backpack and pedaling away.

FRIDAY

I finally gather the courage to pick myself up from the dirt I've been lying in. My face is wet, and I'm sweating in the heat. I get my water bottle from my backpack and drink from it greedily.

Andy's name deserves to be on the rock. *And now it is,* I think.

I stare at his name for a long second. It's a sweet kind of sadness, but I do feel a bit better. I did what I needed to do.

Making my way out of the woods, I hear the birds and feel the heat, but it's almost as if it's happening to someone else— like only the husk of me is present and my mind is somewhere else entirely. I get back on my bike and I realize I'm shaking. My hands quiver as they grip the handlebars. I take another drink of water to wet my mouth and throat, and I'm off again, pedaling south this time.

Finally, I slow to a stop in front of a house I haven't visited in a long while. The Mayrs' house.

I take a deep breath and approach the door, ringing the doorbell. I don't know what to think, so I do my best to think of nothing at all.

EARLIER SATURDAY NIGHT, A MEMORY THREE MONTHS AGO

I pedal home in the cold, late-night air. I pull up to my house and look at its darkened windows, but I don't go in. Instead, I turn and head across the street. I don't want to be alone right now. I want to talk to Shanna.

I gingerly let myself in through the back door of her house. The glow from her TV illuminates the basement; I see her sleeping on the couch, still wrapped tightly in her layers upon layers of blankets.

"Shanna?" I whisper. She doesn't answer, doesn't even stir. I sit on a chair next to her. She looks peaceful. I'm jealous. She might be ill, but I'd trade any fever for how I'm feeling now.

I decide it would be weird if I stay any longer, so I write her a note. "Stopped by, you were sleeping," it reads. "Feel better."

I climb back up the stairs and cross into her front yard, but I'm still not ready to go home. Some part of me knows that, when I'm alone in my own bed, the thoughts won't stop coming.

So I sit on the decorative bench in Shanna's front yard and, not for the first time, realize exactly how tired I am. Pulling my hood up, I close my eyes. It's been a long night, but I'm exhausted, and I fall asleep quickly.

A while later, I'm woken from a fitful slumber. If I dreamed, I don't remember what about. Shanna is standing in front of me in the hazy twilight fog, still cocooned in her blankets.

"What're you doing out here?" she asks, concerned.

"What?" I ask groggily.

"Why're you sleeping in my front yard?"

I stretch, muscles hurting from the cold and from sleeping on the hard bench. "Rough night," I answer tiredly.

"Looks like it. How was the bonfire?" Shanna asks.

I think for a second, about the fire and the people. About Andy. "It was okay until the end," I tell her, miserable.

Shanna sits on the bench next to me. "What happened at the end?"

"Andy told me he's going to college."

"Morgantown?" she asks, surprised.

"No. Some college in Connecticut. I didn't ask which one."

"Oh, Sam," she says. "I'm . . . I don't know. Sorry, I guess."

"Don't be," I tell her. "It's what he wants."

"Still," she insists. "Are you doing okay?"

"Why wouldn't I be?" I say with a glum shrug. She pulls her arm out from under the blankets and wraps it around me, leaning her head on my shoulder. "Who's the one feeling crappy now?" I ask, and she laughs.

"We both are," she says. "Just for different reasons."

We sit like that for a bit, me chilly in the early morning air, Shanna wheezing uncomfortably next to me. I feel a little better, and I tell her it's time for me to go home. My watch says it's almost 5:00 a.m.

"Hang in there, Sam," she calls out behind me as I cross the street.

───────────

I've never been a quiet person, but I might be able to sneak inside and head to bed without being caught. Cracking the front door as silently as possible, I let myself in.

I've misjudged it. Mom and Dad are sitting at the table with the light on, cold cups of coffee on the table in front of them. Mom looks pale and shaky, on the verge of tears. Dad looks tense and angry. They both look up at me as I come in the door. Dad motions to a chair.

"Where have you been?" he asks. I go to respond, but he makes it clear it's a rhetorical question. "Sit down," he commands.

FRIDAY

There's a long beat between when I ring the doorbell and when someone answers it. The sound of the door creaking open is so familiar that I expect to see Andy when it swings wide. But I don't—instead, behind the door is Mrs. Mayr. She looks up and grins widely.

"Sam!" she exclaims. "It's been so long. I've always hoped you'd come by." She steps onto the small porch and hugs me tightly for a long second before letting go and looking up at me. "You're so tall," she says. "I'd forgotten how tall you are."

As she looks up into my face, I look down into hers. Her forehead has lines I don't recall being there, and her hair is duller than the vibrant shade of copper I remember. Frowning, she asks, "Is something wrong? Why aren't you in school?"

"That's, uh, pretty complicated, actually," I tell her, fists clenched tightly by my side. "I couldn't go today. I thought—" I clear my throat. "I thought maybe I could come here, instead."

"Of course!" she tells me. "Come in, please. I'm so glad you've stopped by. Make yourself at home." She leads me up a short flight of stairs and into the kitchen, where she puts a kettle of water on the stovetop. "Do you like tea?" Tittering, she says, "I feel like boys your age don't drink tea, but I can't live without it."

She goes to the pantry and pulls out a box of lemon cookies, which she offers to me. I don't feel well, don't think I can eat, but I take one anyway to be polite. She gives me a napkin and I put it under the cookie, which I set on the table untouched.

"Bella loves these things," she says, motioning toward the cookies. "I wish she were here so you could see her; she's shot up like a beanstalk. She misses you. I hope you'll come by again. She must have grown three inches in the last three months—still dancing, too, but I think she might trade that for soccer soon." She catches herself. "I don't mean to hog the conversation. How have you been?"

"Okay," I say. "Mom is . . . doing okay. Dad, I don't talk to much. He's spending the weekend at the casino."

"Your birthday weekend? And your eighteenth birthday, at that." I'm surprised she remembers, and she must see that on my face. "What, you thought I'd forgotten?" She laughs. "You've spent too many birthdays here for me to forget if I tried. In fact," she continues, "I thought that might be why you came today."

"I don't understand?" I ask, confused.

"To pick up your birthday gift, of course. Did you think we wouldn't get you anything? You're part of our family, Sam. And family celebrates together." As she goes to another room to fetch something, I think back to my pile of opened birthday cards, the ones from my family that I hadn't opened. I feel a knot in my throat now, to accompany the one in my stomach. Mrs. Mayr returns and hands me a lump of wrapping paper.

"Bella wrapped it," she explains. "She wrapped it with love and a *lot* of tape. I told her a little goes a long way, but she had fun with it." The paper is a dark blue, and I open it slowly, not sure what I'll find. Inside is a baseball.

"Happy birthday, Sam. You're eighteen!" Her voice is bright, but it catches like she might be just a little bit sad too.

I feel a flood of emotions and choke up, my eyes fogging. Clutching the ball tightly, I clear my throat and look at Mrs. Mayr.

"Can we talk?" I ask abruptly.

She must see something in my face, because she gives a serious nod. "Come to the living room," she says, leading me toward a faded green sofa next to a recliner. Sitting on the recliner, she directs me to the sofa. "What's going on, Sam?"

I look down at the baseball I'm holding tightly. "I think I did it," I say, voice cracking with emotion. "I think I killed Andy."

EARLY SUNDAY MORNING, A MEMORY THREE MONTHS AGO

I seat myself at the kitchen table in front of my mom and my dad. I don't know what's going on, but there's an anxious air in the house I can't shake, a feeling that something terrible has happened. Dad clears his throat.

"I'm not going to sugarcoat this. Early this morning, they found Andy's body at the northern edge of town."

My extremities go numb. I can't feel my hands or my feet.

"He was the victim of a hit and run. We believe he was either on or near the side of the road when someone struck him with a vehicle. We've been working to identify a driver, but we haven't had any success. Unless someone comes forward, it's very possible we never will."

I don't say anything.

"Do you understand what I'm telling you?" Dad asks.

"Andy is . . . dead?" I say, numb. "How?"

"I told you. Hit and run."

"Forever?" I ask. "Not just to Connecticut?"

Dad ignores me. "You'll come to the station tomorrow to give a statement. Go to bed. You'll need the sleep," he says coldly.

I look at Mom, and see tears in her eyes.

It all slides into a pool then, a murky morass of time. I don't know what happened the rest of that night, or the couple of days afterward. I think I went to the station. I think I told the cops what I knew. I'd left the shack, gone to Shanna's. Fallen asleep. I don't know when Andy left the woods. I don't know.

I don't know.

I didn't know.

———————

Life started up again, slowly at first. Dad was home even less than he had been before. I think he hated me even more now, more than he had previously. I didn't blame him for it. I hated myself.

Finally, things got back up to speed, and I was left behind. I couldn't get out of bed. I couldn't shower, couldn't pay attention in class. Everyone pitied me. No one wanted to help.

Three months of this, until my eighteenth birthday. Eighteen years, and the only birthday present I wanted was to not exist anymore.

That's what I wished for when I blew out my candles. *Let me disappear,* I begged.

Instead, the opposite happened. When I went to sleep on Sunday night, I woke up on Friday again.

I didn't understand it—didn't know what was happening. At first I thought I'd dreamed it, but then it happened and happened again. Mondays, Tuesdays, Wednesdays, Thursdays—they simply weren't anymore. My entire existence was Friday to Sunday, Friday to Sunday, never ending, never ceasing. I couldn't figure out why. I told myself it was because of my dad, tried to reason my way out of it. He was dead, he died on Sunday night, and now his responsibility was my curse. Protect the town. Make it good. Atone for someone else.

But it never quite worked. No matter how hard I tried, I could never worm-logic my way out of it. It wasn't my father—that was only something I told myself so I could avoid the truth.

Three months until my eighteenth birthday, the day I become a man. Three days after my birthday to take responsibility, then another three days, and another three days, until I finally get it right.

I haven't been quite honest with you. I'm sorry it's taken us so long to get here. It's taken meeting Ashley. It's taken hitting rock bottom. It's taken everything I have. Bad duck, me. But now you'll know the truth.

FRIDAY

The color drains from Mrs. Mayr's face.

"I don't understand. You weren't there when Andy died?"

"I wasn't," I tell her. "But I was there beforehand. We had a fight, a *huge* fight, and I was angry at him. So angry, I stormed off. When I went to leave the woods, I—I cut the brakes on his bike."

My voice is shaking. "I didn't hit him with the car, but I didn't have to. If I hadn't done that, I think he would still be here. I *know* he would still be here. The only reason it wasn't found out is because of my dad. He must have done something to cover it up."

Slowly, Mrs. Mayr stands and walks to the kitchen, where the tea kettle is screaming. I'm not sure what to do, so I follow her. With quivering fingers, she puts a bag of tea in a mug, pouring water into the cup.

She turns to me. There's a long second as she clears her throat. She's not looking at me. Her whole body has started to tremor.

"Sam, I need to make sure I heard you correctly," she says, trying to keep her emotions in check. "You're saying you had an argument, and you purposely cut the brake lines on Andy's bike? And—and that's why he—" She falters.

"It was—" I start, but I'm not here to make excuses. "Yes," is all I can bring myself say. My throat has closed up.

Sobs begin, and she clutches her hand to her face. "Why would you do that? You *loved* him."

"I—I still do," I choke out. Mrs. Mayr picks up the mug and sits at the table, face buried in her hands as sobs wrack her body. I don't know what else to do, so I stand in my shame and cry with her.

Guilt-wracked, soul-sick, beyond miserable, we stay like that for what could be two minutes or two hours. It feels like forever, this horrible, wretched in-between space, stomach on fire, nerves twisting.

Finally, the sobs slow. Then, eventually, Mrs. Mayr speaks.

"Why are you telling me this now?" she asks, voice heavy with emotion.

I answer honestly. She deserves that.

"It took . . . a *lot* for me to tell you. More than it should have. I haven't been able to forgive myself. It makes me sick, that I've done—" I struggle for words in all this emotion. "Evil," I finish, spitting it out.

Mrs. Mayr doesn't look at me. I hate myself. *Bad duck,* I think. "I don't expect forgiveness. I don't—I don't even *want* forgiveness. I don't deserve it. I just think you—you deserve to know. And you deserve to know that I'm—I'm *sorry.*" I'm trying to keep it together, but the words are coming faster now, all in a rush, voice cracking. "Not that it matters, or that it counts for anything, 'sorry' won't bring Andy back, but I still want to say it, I *need* to say it, I *need* to tell you that I'm sorry that I hurt you. That I . . . hurt *him*."

There's a long moment of silence then, like something falling through the air in the second before it hits the ground. I hold my breath, waiting for it to break.

"I want to hate you, Sam. For what you did." *There it is,* I think.

"I deserve it," I say numbly.

"Listen to me. I want to hate you"—she takes a ragged breath—"but I can't."

There's another long pause, her hands gripping the table so desperately her knuckles are white. "Anger is a decision. Forgiveness is a decision." There's a long beat as she looks up at me, making eye contact for the first time since I confessed. "So, I forgive you, Sam," she says slowly, face contorting with emotion.

I step back. "No, no, *please* don't—"

"That's not your decision to make. It's mine."

"I don't want it!" I cry out. "I don't deserve it."

"Samuel," she says firmly, her voice still heavy. Releasing her hands from the table, she wipes tears from her cheek. "No one ever does. That's how it works. But I know you, inside and out. I know how much you love my son. I know—"

Her voice catches like she's going to cry again. Instead, she does her best to compose herself, keeping it together. "I know you would never do anything to hurt Andy, not intentionally, and I know what happened has been eating you to death, every single day." She takes another breath, steeling herself. "Telling me was the right thing. Thank you for that. Forgiveness, it—" her voice falters, and she starts again. "It doesn't change the past," she says. I nod mutely. Mrs. Mayr starts to cry again as she speaks. "But, Sam, you are part of my family. I've known you since you were tiny and loved you like my own. I can't change what happened, I can't bring Andy back, but I *can* make the choice to not lose another son. And *that* is my decision."

I hang my head and cry.

Mrs. Mayr envelops me again, squeezing me tightly like her contact can convince me of how much she means her words, words that I don't deserve. Then she hands me a mug of tea and motions for me to sit at the table.

Through our tears and our smiles, we talk about Andy. How much we love him. His grin and his laugh, his easy jokes. His big ideas and plans for the future, his past. Every story we tell, every memory we recall, it's like he's here with us at the kitchen table, perched on the edge of a chair, laughing along with us. And at that table we bring him back to life, if only for an afternoon.

————————

I leave before Bella comes home from school—I don't think I'm ready to see her yet. But I promise Mrs. Mayr I'll be back again. When I get home, Mom is concerned and asks me where I've been. When I tell her the truth, she gives me a long hug.

I lie in bed that night, and for the first time in a long time, I think I'm almost okay. Eventually, I sleep.

EPILOGUE

I wake a long while later. My alarm clock says it's almost a quarter past seven. I shiver from the cold.

Cold? I think, confused and drowsy. *I haven't been cold in—* Months.

I sit upright, not daring to hope, not daring to think.

Running downstairs, I barrel over to the calendar, the calendar in the kitchen, the one with the chickens, the one that says it's—

March.

The first Friday of March, to be exact. The day before it all went bad.

I stare at it stupidly for a long second before I turn and run upstairs, pulling my clothes on, grabbing my backpack, then slamming open my bedroom door, almost colliding with Mom in the hallway. There's a wordless moment before I drop my backpack, then rush in and give her a tight hug.

"Mom, I missed you," I tell her, choking out the words. It doesn't make sense. I don't care.

"Are you all right?" she asks, concerned, held fast in my embrace. I let go and swallow hard.

"I'm . . . I'm okay. I—I need to go." I rush down the stairs and out the door.

Picking up my bike, I streak through the cold morning air. My feet *thump, thump, thump* the pedals as I pedal faster, faster, wind in my hair, brain on the fritz. I don't think, *can't* think, can't let myself think, all the way to school.

Skidding to a stop, I drop my bike into the rack. My stomach is churning, my eyes scan back and forth, back and forth, searching for one student in particular. I see—

Someone else, instead. It's Ashley, hands in her pockets.

I don't know what I'm doing, but I do it anyway. I walk up behind her.

"Hi, Ashley."

Turning around, she's confused. "Hi," she says. *Of course,* I think. *We haven't spoken much before this.* "Do you . . . need something?"

"I do, actually—need something. I need to . . ." I take a deep breath. "To tell you that I think you're really cool, and that you're really good at English. And probably a lot of other things too. And, honestly—" Unable to stop myself, I run my fingers through my hair. "I'd like to be a little more like that. So, I was wondering if you might be able to, I don't know— help me with my geometry homework sometime?"

She takes a step back, cat eyes blinking. There's a long pause.

"Sam Riley, why are you asking me this?"

I swallow hard. "Because I wish I'd done it months ago."

She shoulders her backpack. After a beat, she asks, "Are you good at geometry?"

"I'm terrible," I tell her.

"Good," she says. "Because I like a challenge."

She pulls a pen and a worn notebook from her backpack, and I write down my home phone number. When I hand her back the pen, I realize just how tightly I've been clutching it. "I'll call you," she says, giving me a long look before heading inside.

I step back, letting the novelty of the cold morning air rush over me, making me shiver.

And in that moment, I hear a voice from behind me. A familiar voice.

My throat catches. I can't breathe. I might not breathe ever again.

"Hey, Sam. Finally get another tutor?" the voice asks.

As I begin to turn around, for the first time in forever, I feel something in my stomach that isn't anxiety, or worry, or grief, or anger. It's something new.

Hope, I think. And I let myself believe.

ABOUT THE AUTHOR

Abigail Stark is an author by passion and an engineer by trade. She has more hobbies than talents—while she knows you'd enjoy her writing and cooking, she hopes you never have to hear her sing. She lives in Minneapolis with her husband and dog, who are her biggest fans (and critics, for both her written works and oral performances).